BIRDS OF A FEATHER

A FUC ACADEMY STORY

SCARLET FOX

ACKNOWLEDGMENTS

Thank you to my friends, family, and fans for always supporting me. You mean more to me than I could ever say.

Thank you to Jessica Ripley for the help with the edits and rearranging of things. You always help the flow and point out the kinks that need working out.

Thank you to Devin Govaere for the final read-through and suggestions. Your insight is invaluable and I enjoy reading your comments.

Thank you to Rebecca Pool for the beautiful cover art. Your talents always amaze me.

And thank you to Eve Langlais, for creating this world and not only allowing others to play in it, but supporting and encouraging us to keep going! This is my fourth book in the F.U.C. world and I couldn't be happier to be given the chance to bring the readers another story!

1

———

Broca's aphasia.

The medical diagnosis for what Gabrielle Crowe had been experiencing resembled a cruel nightmare. It was a type of brain damage brought on by the crazy experiments thought up by a pair of deranged minds: Sandy and Dr. Grimm.

The pair of evil researchers had abducted Gabby last year. She and many other birds—including her dad—were held in their underground compound where the scientists attempted to break down a shifter's transformation. The results were horrific. Many were stuck in various stages of the change to bird form. Some were stuck with bird legs, others with bird heads or eyes. Some were completely in bird form but could speak a few words. While Sandy toyed with the language centers in Gabby's brain, Dr. Grimm had other plans. FUC and ASS were able to mount a rescue before Gabby learned of his diabolical plan.

When she was first rescued, it took the doctors a bit to realize what the problem with her language was. It took them even longer to figure out that her mind worked fine. Though she could think fine and understand others, when she tried to communicate, it came out all wrong. Something happened on the journey of language from her brain to her tongue, or hand if she was writing. Even more annoying, she sometimes confused yes with no. Sometimes she could utter a word or two, but none of the doctors of WANC—the Working and Administration Networking Core at the Furry United Coalition Newbie Academy, or FUCN'A, for short— could comprehend what she was trying to say.

The worst, though, was trying to tell the agents that, while they'd arrested Sandy, the red-tailed hawk shifter, Sandy hadn't been alone in her actions. Dr. Grimm, who was also involved, was still at large. When they told her Sandy had been captured, all she could say was, "No."

They reassured her that no one would harm her again. She wished they could understand that she was trying to tell them Sandy wasn't the only evil doctor in the underground lab. Dr. Grimm was still on the loose, and no one knew, aside from her and maybe a few others who probably couldn't communicate either.

Not that Gabby didn't keep trying to tell them. First, she repeated "no," trying to get them to understand she wasn't safe. Then "Grimm." Finally, "Grimm. Out." But no one, not even her little brother, Phineas, could understand what she was trying to say.

Eventually, she gave up. She'd wait until she could talk. But what if he came for her?

Dr. Grimm told Gabby she was special. Even the memory of his thin voice sent ice through her veins. The hair on her neck stood up just thinking about him. Sandy had said he was only interested in Gabby, though Gabby didn't understand why. All she knew that to mean was, odds were, no one else had encountered him. No one else knew about him. No one else would tell FUC about him.

Months went by. Then half a year. And finally a year. Dr. Grimm hadn't come for her. Relief flooded her at the thought. *Maybe he's forgotten about me.* She could only hope. Except Dr. Grimm didn't seem like the forgetting type.

Most nights, Gabby found herself screaming into her hospital pillow, trying to let out the frustration so she wouldn't risk exploding on an unexpecting nurse or doctor. True she had no outward disfigurement, unlike many of the other experiments, and should consider herself lucky. Guilt was a prickly heaviness inside of her whenever her frustrations rose at her inability to communicate. Her situation could have been worse. But to Gabby, living trapped in her own body seemed a cruel fate. No, that was too dramatic a statement. She could at least move around. Walk. Try to communicate in other ways. It was just that her leaden tongue messed up everything she tried to say. Her train of thought was fine, but somewhere along the track, the cars jumbled out of order and only one of them made it to her mouth. Often the correct word didn't even come out. Sometimes she said the opposite of what she intended.

Gabby steeled herself to settle in and start her evening ritual. It wasn't that she didn't like therapy or the homework exercises she was assigned. In fact, Lynn, her cognitive thera-pist, courtesy of FUC—the Furry United Coalition—was very nice and patient. She taught Gabby word games she could complete on her own to build up her ability to speak and write again. Lynn also encouraged Gabby to challenge her negative thoughts. Instead of allowing negative thoughts to linger, such as "I will never talk again" or "I'm stupid," Gabby learned to replace them with hopeful ones, such as, "This is going to take time, and that's okay." Though most days, it felt anything but okay.

Her father, Joe, was probably the only one who understood what she was going through. She only wished she could commiserate with him. Alas, she'd given up on the idea of doing normal things with her father again. Hell, she didn't think she'd ever see him in human form for more than a few minutes.

Along with Gabby, Joe was captured and changed by Sandy and Dr. Grimm. FUC and ASS—the Avian Soaring Security rescued Joe from the same underground lab as Gabby and the others. Like Gabby, her father had difficulty speaking—could only utter one or two words at a time. However, Joe's situation differed greatly. Unlike Gabby, who looked human, her father was stuck in crow form. The doctors and specialists at WANC had been able to get him to change back into human form only briefly. It was better than nothing, Gabby supposed.

She felt horrible feeling so low about her own situation when things could be so much worse. As much sympathy as she had for him, she also realized that she had to grieve for the father she'd lost.

The two of them weren't the only ones facing challenges, though. Most of the patients on her floor came from the same lab. Some of them were in worse shape than Gabby and her dad. The other day, she saw a man with a human body and a bird head. What a terrible sight to see! What was worse, the pang of guilt quickly set in after Gabby realized seeing him made her feel better about her own situation. That sting of shame curled up inside her gut just thinking about it. What a selfish thought, to feel better after seeing someone else's injuries.

Gabby reached behind her, grabbing her trusty pillow. She squeezed it with her fingers. *This is soft.* Her cognitive therapist encouraged her to try shorter sentences. "S-soft. Soft. It," came out instead. Still wrong. But close. Her therapist would be proud that she focused on the positive instead of the negative.

She tried to smile, but it wouldn't come. It felt stuck, like her words. A hot tear stung at the corner of her eye, blurring her vision. Gabby put the pillow to her face and screamed.

The strange noise sounded again. Lyla Cruiz woke up from a dead sleep and shot up in her hospital bed, glancing around for any sign of an intruder. Nothing seemed out of place, aside from the sound. A muffled, guttural cry coursed down the hall. She hopped out of bed and tiptoed toward her door, peering out. Nurses and other staff milled about as if nothing was awry.

Am I hearing things? She didn't think so. She heard a similar noise yesterday and a gagged sniffle last week. It laced through the nights, reminding her too much of the sounds from her cell at the lab. Other experiments crying themselves to sleep. When she first arrived at WANC, Lyla thought it was a memory, etched in her brain, playing on repeat until she fell asleep. It was never loud though, which made her question if it was real. But the more she analyzed it, the more she decided it had to be one of the patients. If it was a memory cropping up, wouldn't it always be the same volume? This sound changes pitch, tone, and intensity. If Lyla didn't investigate, her brain would drive her crazy running through all the scenarios or what it could be.

She leaned out the doorway further, feeling a tug at her hand. The IV line stretched taut behind her. Lyla trudged back to the bed, grabbing the metal rack that held the dextrose solution drip. It snaked its way down a plastic tube all the way to her left hand. She stuck her tongue out at it. If she had to spend another month in the hospital dealing with the tests, medicine, and being poked and prodded, she would scream.

Wait! That's it, that's the noise. Someone is screaming. But who?

Lyla couldn't sit around another night, pretending it wasn't happening. Determination puffed up her chest. She was sick of being scared. This wasn't the dank cell she was used to. It was a hospital. "I'm safe," she reminded herself as she rolled the IV bag next to her like a trusty companion. "Sorry for earlier," she said to the bag. "I didn't mean it." She gave it a shy smile.

For months before coming to the FUCN'A hospital, Lyla had no one to talk to, and in that time, she'd picked up the terrible habit of talking to inanimate objects. Though it was deeper than that, and she knew it. She really *did* feel bad about sticking her tongue out at the bag, as if it had its own feelings. Definitely not normal, but it had helped her to survive the last half a year in the tiny cell she'd called home.

It wasn't the experiments that bothered her as much as the isolation. Lyla came from what some would consider a big family. The silence of her cell had gnawed at her brain until, out of desperation for company, she befriended a tiny pebble on the floor. She kept that tidbit of information to herself when the psychiatrist at WANC evaluated her soon after her rescue, but she had brought her old friend with her to the hospital. The grey stone now sat at her bedside table, and she explained to the staff that it was more than a souvenir. It was proof she survived. If anyone noticed it and found it odd, they never said. Lyla glanced back at it long-ingly. She wished she had a pocket to take her trusty rock with her, but alas, the simple T-shirt and shorts FUCN'A provided offered no such luxury. At least they were better than the hospital gown she'd had to wear when she was first treated. That thing barely covered her ass.

Lyla popped her head back into the hallway before taking a bounding step out into it. She nodded to the nurses she passed, plastering a smile on her face. "Out for an evening stroll?" one of them asked.

"You know me. Staying in my room for too long feels like I'm back in that cell." *Or a bird in a cage.* Plus, all that hummingbird energy gave her cabin fever. Pacing the halls was far better than pacing her room. And seeing others out and about helped quell the loneliness.

The nurse nodded. "Just let us know if you need anything." She went back to the paperwork in front of her as if not hearing the muffled screams that had pulled Lyla from her room to investigate.

Why didn't anyone else seem to hear the noise? It sounded like a wounded animal or someone in extreme mental anguish. Maybe both. In a hospital full of shifters and people who were experimented on, it could be anything.

Maybe they all know who it is. Did that person ask to be left alone? Lyla wondered. She certainly didn't think the staff ignored the noise because they were cruel. The people at FUCN'A were anything but.

Once again, she wondered if she was somehow the only one who could hear it… which was why she simply thanked the nurse before continuing on in the direction she believed the sound was coming from. Until shew knew it was real and not just in her head, she wouldn't say a word of it. To anyone.

But she couldn't keep trying to ignore it. *I need to know who's screaming.*

Suddenly, the sounds stopped. So did she. Lyla pretended to adjust her hospital sock as a doctor walked by. It would look odd if she just stood in the hallway, staring at nothing, doing nothing.

A sob echoed out of one of the rooms up on the left. Lyla shuffled her feet forward, afraid to scare off whatever, or whoever, it was. She peeked into the room. The patient appeared to be sound asleep, their long trunk—literally, a long elephant trunk replaced their nose—quivering with a snore. *Was that it? Am I mistaken?* Lyla scratched at her head, ruffling up the feathers mixed in with her pink hair.

She dyed her hair pink because it was still her favorite color. When she was a child, her whole room at her mom's house was shades of pink. The feathers adorned her head like a fluffy crown because some whacked-out, evil scientist wanted to see how to change the way shifters looked in human form. And coming out of it with only feathers to show meant she was one of the lucky ones. The sleeping patient before her didn't appear so lucky. Their human face appeared far too small to support the elephant appendage.

Not wanting to linger rudely in the doorway, Lyla decided to press on. After some consideration, she decided the trunk snoring was not the muffled screams she'd heard earlier, so she kept looking for the source. As she shuffled down toward the next room, another nurse rushed by. It was oddly busy for the night shift. *Something must be up.* Maybe there was a fresh delivery of rescued shifters in need of fixing. That was, if they could be fixed. Lyla herself had stumped the docs—none could figure out how to rid Lyla of the feathers sticking out of her head.

She poked her head in the next room. There, a lump of a body lay in bed. Wavy, brown hair flowed out from underneath a pillow. Lyla feared something terrible had happened and was about to call the doctor when she noticed the person's chest rise and fall. They were breathing, at least.

Lyla knocked at the open door, taking a step inside the dark room. "Umm..." She wasn't sure what to say. What was proper etiquette when you walked in on someone with a pillow over their face? She didn't know.

The person startled, popping up like a flower that'd just seen the sun after a week of clouds. Lyla noted that she wasn't just any person. Not just one of a hundred faces that passed through these halls. This was a beautiful woman, clearly startled, and the sight of her made Lyla's breath hitch.

The stranger's fluffy brown hair floated around her like a storm, flowing around her face in a tangled mess that she tried to tame with her fingers. Wide blue eyes fixed on Lyla, and Lyla's heart skipped a beat when their eyes locked. She tried to ignore the flutter of butterflies in her stomach and remember why she was actually out and about. Now that she'd discovered the source of the sound, she could return to her room. Mystery solved.

"I should go." The words went against every fiber of her being. She wanted to stay, to find out why this woman screamed every night, but what if she was intruding?

"Okay," the woman agreed. But when Lyla turned to go, she said, "No."

The woman's firm voice stopped Lyla in her tracks.

She turned toward the woman's tear-streaked face. "You *don't* want me to go?" Lyla wasn't sure what to do. Which was it? Go or stay? She had to admit to herself she didn't mind sticking around. It seemed that whoever they were and whatever had happened to them, they needed a friend.

The patient nodded her head then quickly shook it. "No."

What the heck? Lyla raised an eyebrow. She crossed the room toward the bed, plucking the patient's chart from the end of it. Nosiness be damned because confusion got the best of her. Okay. Maybe some curiosity, too. She hoped the person didn't mind. Lyla glanced up from the chart before opening it, wondering if the woman would stop her from taking a peek. The woman only blinked at her.

Though "woman" didn't quite describe her. She looked just out of her teens, a few years younger than Lyla. Twenty-one years old according to her chart. "Broca's aphasia," she read off of the paperwork, glancing up at the woman who looked back at her with sheer curiosity. *Right. I have feathers sticking out of my hair.* "They're my souvenir from Sandy," Lyla explained with a snicker as she waved one hand around her head, pretending to fluff the sparse plumage. "What's Broca's aphasia?" she asked the woman in the hospital bed—whose name was Gabrielle, according to the chart Lyla probably shouldn't be reading.

"Speech. N-not." Gabrielle's brow wrinkled up in frustration. She bit her lip, slamming her fists down on the bed next to her.

Lyla crossed the room, IV bag in tow, to put a reassuring hand on her shoulder. "Can't speak well. I got it." She kept her words soft, using the same reassuring tone she used to give her younger brother when he failed a new skateboarding move he was trying to pull off.

Gabrielle's shoulders deflated with a sigh as relief flooded her pale face. She glanced up at Lyla. "Gabby." She pressed a hand to her chest, the shadow of a smile on her face.

Lyla noted that though Gabby struggled to talk, she seemed to understand Lyla just fine. *Poor thing.* Lyla heard some of the doctors talking about birds speaking words, but she didn't know too much more about the other rescued experiments. A lot of them came from a big bust last year. A few were from the small lab where Lyla was kept. As far as she knew, both were run by Sandy, a demented scientist who thought messing up people's lives and splicing genes that probably shouldn't be mixed was cool. An asshole move, if you asked Lyla.

"I'm Lyla." She decided to introduce herself to her new friend. If she did most of the talking, maybe she could keep Gabby company and frustration-free. It seemed trying to talk and having the wrong words come out led to Gabby's agitation. Maybe even the nightly screaming. "I'm a hummingbird shifter. I'm a recent addition here. I was rescued by FUC 'n ASS a few weeks ago."

Gabby started giggling, which was a beautiful and much-improved sound from her distraught neighbor.

Lyla chuckled herself. "So you find the acronyms as ridiculous as I do." Lyla cast a glance at her IV pole. "I told you so," she said to the bag without meaning to say it out loud. When Gabby stopped laughing, Lyla inhaled sharply.

Gabby didn't say anything, but Lyla offered an explanation anyway. "I was kept alone for a while. I'm sure you know what it's like." She picked at the skin on the side of her fingernail before getting the courage to look back up at Gabby.

Gabby nodded. "No." She wrinkled up her cute little nose. "No," she repeated before throwing up her hands in frustration.

"It's okay," Lyla reassured her. "You get words mixed up. Sometimes say the opposite of what you mean?"

Gabby nodded after shaking her head.

"That has to be so irritating. No wonder you scream into your pillow every night."

A rosy blush crept across Gabby's pale cheeks. She looked mortified that Lyla knew about the screaming.

"I'm sorry. I just…" Lyla felt a similar heat in her face. She was going to explain when she heard a nurse down the hall calling her name. She glanced at the IV bag. The drip was almost out. It wouldn't be long before a nurse found her.

While she knew they were okay with her walking alone, she wasn't sure how they'd feel after finding out she'd perused through another patient's chart. Especially a patient who was maybe unable to protest her doing so.

"I have to go." She gestured apologetically toward her IV bag. "I'm in room 102 down the hall. Feel free to stop by."

Without a backward glance, Lyla rushed out of the room, pressing a cool palm to her burning cheek. She'd looked like such a crazy person. Feathers sticking out of her head aside, she'd talked to her IV bag in front of someone. A very cute someone. She wished she could've melted into the floor.

"Lyla," Nurse Mya chided, gripping the full dextrose solution bag in her hand. "I've been looking all over for you." Her high-pitched voice rang down the hallway. Her words suggested she might be upset with Lyla, but the smile on her face contradicted that. Mya could never be properly mad, even if she tried.

The IV stand rolled along, Lyla's anchor and friend of sorts. Embarrassment grew as Lyla felt all eyes on her. She felt like a kid caught outside of class when she should've been studying. "I'm sorry."

"It's okay," the nurse reassured her. A smile spread across her face. Lyla didn't know how the nurse kept up such good spirits working in the rehab wing. "We just need to keep your sugar up." The fluorescent lights glowed on Mya's dark brown skin, bouncing off her round cheeks. She had a motherly face, bordering on angelic.

As a hummingbird shifter, sugar was important to Lyla's diet. And the jerks who kept her locked in a cell didn't give a damn about that. Lyla's energy was almost back to normal, but it took a constant glucose drip to keep it that way for the moment. Part of Lyla couldn't wait to be free of the IV bag, yet another part felt she would miss the constant company. *It's not a living, breathing being,* she reminded herself. She fought the urge to apologize to the IV bag for the slight against it.

Lyla followed Mya back into her tiny room. "You going to the party this weekend?" Mya asked, pointing at a flyer on the wall for one of the parties Huggie Gibeault, the Campus Activities Coordinator, was hosting. The fisher shifter tried her best to keep the atmosphere light, allowing everyone a break from their hospital beds. Lyla heard some of the parties were for staff and cadets, too. A nice way to mingle. Getting to know some of the other survivors might not be such a bad idea, especially if Gabby was going... It would be an even better way to get to know her. If anyone needed a friend in this place, it was Gabby.

"I may," Lyla responded as she reached her door. She shuffled her feet across the floor for fun before settling down into bed. Mya switched out the empty bag for the new one. The coolness of the liquid entered her veins. She wondered how she didn't notice the sensation had stopped when the fluid ran out.

"Can I go to the computer lab tomorrow?" Lyla wanted to learn more about Gabby's condition and her family wasn't supposed to visit until next week. She had plenty of time on her hands. Plus maybe it would help Lyla to talk Gabby into going to Huggie's party. Plus, maybe she could figure out a better way to talk with Gabby. Watching the torment of her trying to speak was excruciating. Lyla knew it wasn't her fault, but she still felt bad watching Gabby's frustration grow. If she could find a way to ease their communication, it might help her new friend to not want to scream into her pillow nightly. Lyla knew the sound wouldn't bother her as much now that she knew what caused it—and didn't have to fear it was just in her head. On the other hand—or wing—knowing it was Gabby, and knowing it was the sound of mental anguish, would break her heart. Lyla was determined to help her.

"We'll see," Mya said vaguely before leaving the room.

If she wasn't allowed to wander off, the nurse would have given her an outright, "No." Lyla's excitement grew. It buzzed in her chest. At this rate, she wouldn't sleep at all. It would give her time to think of a way to help Gabby. She thought back to Gabby's messy hair. It was somehow beautiful, framing her pale face, contrasting with her blue eyes. Lyla shook her head. She couldn't get ahead of herself. First, she'd find a way to lessen Gabby's frustration when talking, and then they'd work on their possible friendship. See where that went. And the party? Who knew if Gabby would feel comfortable going? Or going with Lyla. Butterflies buzzed in Lyla's stomach at the thought of asking her. Nope. One thing at a time. The computer lab was the priority.

For now, she'd have to sleep. "Good night." She patted the IV bag and smiled at her pebble before rolling over. Tomorrow would be a long day. Before she drifted off to sleep, her mind wandered back to Gabby. She wondered what stories she'd tell after being able to talk again.

3

———

Though sleep was easier to find after the unexpected visitor left, Gabby's dreams were filled with experiments gone wrong. Men with bird legs, women with swan necks and human bodies, people in shifter form who could talk. A jumbled mess of terrible memories formed a patchwork of nightmares. Ones she wished she could forget. The images faded upon waking, yet nibbled on her mind, ready to pop back in if anything in the surrounding environment reminded Gabby's brain of her trauma. As Paige—the counselor who met with Gabby soon after she was rescued to evaluate her mental health—put it, PTSD was a normal reaction to not-normal events. Gabby had enough to beat herself up about. She tried to let go of feeling bad about having flashbacks and nightmares and being overly jumpy. Besides, she suspected almost everyone in the rehab wing had some symptoms of PTSD.

Gabby rubbed at the sleep in her eyes, dreading what the morning would bring. Today, she would visit with her father. At least one other person on the planet understood how frustrating it was to be unable to communicate well.

Though that stranger last night, Lyla, seemed to get it. And quickly. Gabby's heart had melted when Lyla reassured her. It was an odd sensation and one Gabby chalked up to not having very many understanding friends around her. Though they weren't together long, Gabby found Lyla easy to be around. She felt she could be herself around Lyla, which wasn't something she was used to. At the hospital, some days it felt like only her progress—or lack thereof—was measured. That she, as a person, wasn't seen. She was expected to perform and show what was getting easier when, most days, it felt like nothing was. But around Lyla, she'd felt no pressure.

"Are you ready?" Lynn, her cognitive therapist, popped her head into Gabby's room. She gnawed on the pencil she kept with her, waiting for Gabby to respond. Gabby wondered if the beaver shifter needed wood to chew on at all times. She once heard a rumor that if beavers didn't continuously chew on things, their teeth would keep growing until they couldn't shut their mouths anymore. She wondered if that affliction affected Lynn's human teeth. The thought brought forth an unpleasant mental image. She shook it out of her mind.

Gabby realized Lynn was staring at her, waiting for a response. She refocused, trying to think of the best response. A reply with a few words—or one word—would do. Lynn's patient eyes softened as Gabby concentrated. She thought, "Yes."

She wanted to say yes… but heard her mouth say, "No." A puff of air blew from Gabby's lips, though she tried not to look defeated. The corners of her mouth shifted in a failed attempt at smiling. So much for staying positive.

"Try singing it," Lynn encouraged. She stuck the pencil behind her ear, pushing back her black hair.

Gabby's eyebrows raised. It was a strange request. Something they hadn't practiced before in session. She decided to go with the rhythm and notes of "Twinkle, Twinkle."

"Yes, yes, yes, yes…" She put her hand up to her lips with a gasp, clamping them over her mouth. *It worked! It actually worked!*

She cocked her head sideways, staring at Lynn as a wide smile spread across her face, this one genuine. It warmed up her soul. Lynn's, too, by the look on her face. Her slightly-longer-than-human central incisors jutted over her lower lip in a tooth-filled grin.

"Singing comes from a different part of the brain," Lynn explained, tapping at the right side of her head. She pulled the pencil from behind her ear and started gnawing on it again. Gabby wondered what would happen if she hit the graphite at the center. Though the outside of the pencil was marred with teeth indents, it didn't look like Lynn ever chewed through it. But who knew, maybe the shifter had a cupboard full of pencils in her office.

Gabby wanted to ask why Lynn didn't lead with singing as a tool for speaking on day one, but figured she had her reasons. Plus, it might be too difficult to try to form that much of a question. Maybe Lynn hadn't wanted Gabby to use it as a crutch and not put in the work of doing the exercises she assigned her. Though Gabby did enjoy her homework. It helped to pass the time. She always enjoyed school and handouts. She wanted to go to university one day—if she was ever able to figure out how to finance it. But that was a problem for another day. Right now, she had to focus on learning to speak and write properly again.

They passed a flyer boasting of a "fun time" plastered on the bulletin board. Gabby'd been pretending they didn't exist. The thought of attempting to talk to others nauseated her. Daily she struggled to communicate. A break from it was rejuvenating. A party would be Hell.

Lynn chuckled as if reading her mind. "I have an idea."

Nervousness fizzed in Gabby's stomach. She saw Lynn's brown eyes roll from the poster on the wall to Gabby. She started shaking her head, not caring that she actually got the gesture correct.

"Yes. I think you should go to the party this weekend. It would be good practice." Lynn went back to chewing on her pencil, nodding to herself.

Gabby's stomach dropped. "I-I…" She pictured the words she wanted hopping on the train that took them from her brain to mouth. "Rather." She screwed up her face in deep concentration. "Rest." That was the closest Gabby had ever gotten to the full sentence. The excitement of her small triumph was quickly squashed by the anxiety that Lynn would force her to attempt interacting with others at the party.

"See! Look at how well you're doing. Imagine how much you'll improve after more practice. At least think about it." Lynn put the pencil back behind her ear after inspecting it. "I knew I should have grabbed a new one today."

Gabby swallowed hard. At least Lynn loosened up a little about the party. She'd have the rest of the week to come up with an excuse not to go. But to the problem at hand…

A pebble of dread solidified in Gabby's chest when she thought about the visit with her dad looming before her. She hated that feeling. Felt guilty it existed. Seeing family was hard when she struggled to talk. Watching her brother's heart break weekly was worse. Their bird-dad was a category all on its own. She felt her shoulders roll forward as she wilted like a flower at the memories of past visits.

"I think you'll be impressed with his progress," Lynn piped up as if reading her thoughts. She led the way down the hall to the family room. Familiar staff nodded in greeting as they passed. Gabby's anxiety grew with each step, buzzing beneath her breastbone before coiling around her heart. "Here we are." Lynn held the door open to the therapy room.

Many experiments came to the facility with amnesia, or at least that was what Gabby had heard. But for those who kept their memories and knew who they were, yet needed to stay on-site for treatment, the family therapy room came in handy for allowing visitations.

Gabby supposed she should be grateful that both she and her father had their memories intact. She wasn't so sure that she was though. She wondered if it would be easier to see him in his current state if she didn't remember who he used to be. It seemed it wouldn't hurt so badly in that case, since she'd have nothing to compare it to.

Guilt squeezed her heart. She should feel lucky that he was alive and safe. Sadness over his current condition shouldn't be there. *Shouldn'ts get us nowhere except upset*, she remembered the counselor, Paige, telling her when she first arrived at WANC.

"I'll be back with the doctor in a bit." Lynn smiled encouragement at her before taking her leave. Her tiny feet padded down the hallway, leaving Gabby with her family. She was afraid for a minute to turn to them. Her anxiety wanted her to leave, but she refused. She couldn't disappoint them like that.

Gabby held her breath, gaining her courage. She turned, expecting to see her bird-dad perched on the arm of one of the sofas lining the walls.

But the anxiety changed to relief when she spotted her father sitting in human form on the couch next to Phin. "Dad!"

Her father's human face lit up in a smile. He had wrapped a robe around his small frame—though he'd always been a small man, the time in the lab had seemed to shrink him— hiding the thin material of the hospital gown beneath that covered his body. His human body. *All* human. No random bird parts. None that Gabby could see anyway.

"Not bird." He shook his head. Joy blossomed inside Gabby at the words. They weren't much, but they meant all the world to her. Just to be able to see her father's face again, his clear blue eyes, his thin lips, the scar across his chin, his arms and legs. She never thought she'd be able to see him like this again. She feared he would be stuck as a bird forever. Joe rose from the couch and wrapped his arms around Gabby, pulling her in for a big hug. Her eyes glistened with tears of happiness. This moment felt too good to be true. Gabby thought her father would never be able to hug her again.

Kristen, their mom, sat on the opposite couch across from Joe. A smile lit up Kristen's face. Gabby's family was comprised of cross-species shifters. Her mother and younger brother were mice, while she and her dad were crows. Their parents had divorced just last year, but they'd kept in contact, being civil for the sake of the kids. Since Gabby and her father had come to FUCN'A, Kristen had been a regular visitor, showing her support for both her daughter and ex-husband—though the latter was for Phin's benefit.

Kristen smiled politely at Joe, pleased by his progress and trying her best to be supportive. Gabby could tell her mom wished she wasn't spending as much time with her ex, but at the same time, would do anything for Phin to be able to see their dad as often as possible. Gabby knew Mom wanted to leave the marriage years before she had. Spending time hanging out with her ex at a hospital was probably the last thing she wanted on her agenda. But whenever Phin had time to come, she brought him to see his sister and father. Sometimes Kristen came on her own, though, just to see Gabby. She would read to her so the pressure wasn't on Gabby to talk. That was really nice and thoughtful. Gabby looked forward to those days.

Phin had just turned eleven, yet somehow last year he'd helped in the rescue of Gabby and their dad. He served as an inspiration to her. If Phin could be that strong emotionally for someone so small, then Gabby could be brave, too… even if most days she felt anything but.

Now Phin skipped over to their mom, and that was when Gabby noticed a bag next to her, hiding behind a throw pillow. Phin smiled from ear to ear.

"I've brought presents," Phin cheered while rummaging through the crinkling paper bag. She loved having Phin around during visiting hours. He always lightened the mood and did most of the talking. Though part of Gabby felt that was so he didn't have to watch her or Joe struggle to talk.

As Phin occupied himself with the bag, Gabby watched his long brown hair bouncing on his shoulders. "Haircut," Gabby said, catching herself talking without realizing it.

Phin rolled his eyes—bright blue ones like their father. "You sound just like mom," he groaned, not realizing how big a deal it was for Gabby to utter those two syllables.

"It's not good to wear your hair in your eyes," Mom chided, crossing her arms as she leaned back into the couch. A ghost of a smile whispered across her lips as she looked at Gabby. She'd know how impressive it was for Gabby to speak, but she also knew that Gabby would become flustered if anyone made a big deal about it.

With a puff of air, Phin blew the strands of hair out of his face. "When it grows long enough, I can tie it back like you." Having found what he was looking for, Phin turned and held out his little hands to both Gabby and their dad. A tiny, plastic crow sat in the center of each palm. "I bought these at a school fair. I thought the size was perfect. Dad can keep it in his beak when he changes back into a crow."

Gabby plucked the miniature version of her shifter form from her brother's hand. A smile spread across her face.

"Thank you, Phin." His thoughtfulness warmed her heart. She'd try to think of this moment the next time she wanted to scream into her trusty pillow.

"You said a whole sentence!" Phin beamed back at her.

"Short. It." Gabby sighed. Maybe she should've just accepted the compliment instead of being reproachful. She didn't know how to react when people praised her for tiny accomplishments, like saying thank you. To her, it didn't feel like progress, though she had to admit that it was.

"It still counts," Phin countered, balling up his tiny fists to put on his hips. He always opposed her need to be perfect.

"Right." Her dad nodded as he took one of the bird figures and turned it over in his hand. Gabby wondered if he felt bad that he wasn't able to say more. Most of his progress had been physical. They hadn't even started trying to figure out how to get him to speak normally again. Maybe he never would.

Suddenly her father's eyes widened, as if in fear. "What's wrong?" Phin asked.

"Change." Before he could attempt to elaborate further in one-word sentences, her father disappeared within the robe. A black-feathered head poked out, rising up from the garment. A *caw* sounded from his beak.

Gabby tilted her head. That was new. Before, her father could also say words as a bird. Did this mean her dad was regressing? She turned to her mom.

"They said they made a lot of progress," Kristen said with a shrug. "Last week he was only human for a minute. This week he made it to almost ten. That's a lot of progress, Gabby."

Gabby wasn't so sure she agreed. Maybe she was just being pessimistic.

Her dad rummaged around in the fabric of the robe. After disappearing for a moment, he popped back up with the plastic crow figurine Phin gave him, bobbing his little bird head. He squawked a muffled sound, excitement perhaps, showing his gratitude for Phin's present.

"Good idea." Gabby fluffed up her brother's hair with her hand. He tried to smile up at her, but only one corner of his mouth rose. She pulled him in for a hug, feeling her heart break all over again. "Kay kay. Okay." *It will be okay,* she wanted to say. Gabby bit her lip, mad she couldn't properly console her brother. Why was it so much easier to speak when she wasn't flustered?

Kristen looked like she was about to say something when the door swung open. Dr. Brown walked in with her clipboard, Lynn in tow Both had wide grins on their faces like they'd won the lottery. Gabby didn't know what all the smiles were about. She couldn't imagine anything to smile about when she was trying her best to hold back tears.

"Joe?" Dr. Brown asked, glancing down at her watch and then at the crow making a nest out of the robe. "That was the longest yet!" Her brown eyes twinkled with triumph.

He glanced up at her with his amber bird eyes before bobbing his head, the toy bird still clutched in his beak.

"What's that?" Lynn asked, looking expectantly at Gabby.

Gabby wished she could transform into her bird form and disappear. Technically, she could—she flew around the atrium three times a week, monitored by Dr. Brown— but she figured the doctor and Lynn wouldn't be pleased she was avoiding the situation. "Gift. Ph-ph-phin. Gift. From."

"Good. Look at how many words you just said." Lynn clasped her hands together before taking her pencil from behind her ear and gnawing on the wood some more. The cognitive therapist scooped up her dad, while Dr. Brown grabbed his garments. "Let's get you back to your room for some more work." Her father bobbed his head, *cawing* excitedly.

Kristen nodded, putting her arms around both Gabby and Phin. "You're both making a lot of progress," she noted, walking back to the couch. The doctor and Lynn left the room after saying their goodbyes, taking Joe and his belongings with them.

"See," she said to her brother who was still in her arms. She brushed the hair out of his eyes. "Okay."

"I just thought you'd both be back to normal by now." Phin dropped his head, walking back to Kristen. His small feet dragged on the floor with each step.

You and me both, kid. Gabby smiled tightly, feeling the sting of tears in her eyes and the back of her throat. She swallowed it down for Phin. He had to know she was okay, even if she wasn't. Tonight, she would need an extra session of screaming into her pillow to decompress. Seeing her dad was always hard. Seeing Phin made it worse. She and Dad were always disappointing him. Her therapist tried to help her see that while the whole situation was sad, Phin was at least happy they'd been rescued, but Gabby couldn't get over her perfectionist tendencies enough to see it that way. She only felt the weight of their failure.

4

Lyla flitted around, enjoying the heat and humidity of the aviary in her hummingbird form. Every day she seemed to have more energy, and each shifted session lasted longer. The less fatigue she had, the longer the doctors allowed Lyla to stay as a hummingbird. Visiting the beautiful flowers was one of her favorite things to do. One small normal thing throughout her rehab where nothing else felt typical.

While Lyla loved the staff, she felt guilty wishing she could be home. Her family lived nearly five hours away from WANC. While they visited as often as they could, Lyla missed them. She knew they were doing the best they could. Her mom and stepdad couldn't afford to take a lot of time off of work to visit.

Lyla also felt her life was put on hold, waiting for her body to fully recover and no longer need doctor supervision. Before the whole ordeal, Lyla had been working as a barista at a coffee shop and saving up to take some online courses in computer programming. She couldn't wait to get back to it. But now her focus had shifted to getting better. She was becoming impatient. Lyla wanted to spread her wings and fly, not stay cooped up in a hospital.

While the Furry United Coalition usually only dealt with *furry* shifters, the recent rescue of Sandy's patients meant they had a large influx of birds, and a family by the name of Goosby had reached out with the idea—and money—for the new structure.

Lyla was thankful for the location. It beat shifting and flying in the gym, that's for sure. Outside was out of the question. Dr. Brown insisted she only be allowed to shift under supervision, and outside provided too many potential hazards.

She wasn't the only bird patient who was enjoying exercise that morning. She saw several others, some flying fast, some slow. A cuckoo was spending most of its time on a branch, and a crane waded through the fountain in the middle of the structure. Lyla avoided crossing paths with the osprey. His hooked beak and sharp talons made her nervous, even if they were all being watched closely at all times.

The dextrose drip must have been doing its job, because Lyla felt she could flutter about in hummingbird form all day if she wanted, though the doctors had warned her against going too long until they knew she was properly nourished. When she'd been in captivity, Lyla wasn't fed as often as she should have been, for any shifter or pure human. The evil scientists were more concerned with their results than the health of their subjects. Or their consent.

"You could burn through all the stored energy if you do too much, too soon," Dr. Brown always cautioned.

Lyla knew this, just as she knew hummingbirds needed a lot of calories since their wings beat so fast. She tried her best not to roll her eyes whenever Dr. Brown reminded her. She was just trying to help.

"That's time, Lyla!" Dr. Brown called.

Her immediate instinct was to fly away in the other direction. To assert her rebellious nature and also show that she had lots more energy to go.

But then she remembered that she wanted to save some of that energy for her trip to the computer lab... and she'd also need to follow instructions if she hoped to be granted a favor. It seemed an easy choice but still challenging, especially when she was getting cabin fever from being cooped up inside for too long.

Reluctantly, she returned to the ground, going behind the curtain that had been set up to allow students to shift and dress in privacy. Nudity wasn't a big deal to shifters, but it was still a considerate gesture.

"That's fifteen minutes more than last week," Dr. Brown announced when she emerged with a triumphant smile. "Let's check your vitals."

Lyla sat down as a nurse slid on the blood pressure cuff and clipped the oxygen meter on her finger. Dr. Brown listened to her heart rate and breathing. Once they were done, another nurse arrived with a tray of sweets for Lyla to replenish herself with. She gobbled up half the chocolate and fruit before Dr. Brown could review her vitals.

"Your stats are looking good," Dr. Brown announced. "I'm really pleased with your progress."

"But not pleased enough to take me off the IV yet?" she asked as one of the nurses approached her with a new one.

"Not quite yet," Dr. Brown replied with a note of regret. "Be patient. I think your treatment is working, even if it does seem slow to a speedy hummingbird like yourself." She gave her a kind smile before she left to check on another of her patients.

The nurse finished setting up her new IV bag and left Lyla to eat and drink. Lyla gulped down the rest of the apple juice on the tray, noting that they usually gave her four glasses of it. Today only two. She took that as a sign she was nearing the end of her recovery, that her body had finally started to produce more energy on its own.

"Lyla, right?" A woman with long silky black hair approached her.

"Yes," she replied cautiously. Paranoia after being abducted and held captive wasn't easy to get rid of. "Who are you?" She eyed up the woman for any hints as to who she was and if she was safe to converse with.

"I'm Agent Nari Lee, from the Avian Soaring Society. Mind if I sit?" Agent Lee indicated the chair next to Lyla.

"Be my guest." Lyla shrugged. She'd met another ASS agent—Cass Sparks—and she'd been nice enough, so Lyla had no reason to be wary of Agent Lee.

"How are things going here?" Agent Lee asked. "Is FUCN'A treating you well?"

"Yeah," Lyla said, tearing off a piece of cookie and popping it into her mouth.

Lee smiled, though it didn't seem to touch her eyes. "I'm glad to hear that. Traditionally, they don't specialize in birds."

Lyla glanced around at the aviary. "They seem to be doing a pretty good job after rescuing all of Sandy's abductees." Referring to herself and the rest as "experiments" seemed wrong. She felt it depersonalized them in some way.

"Have you thought about what you want to do after you recover?" the agent asked, ignoring Lyla's defense of FUC.

"Ahh…" Somehow, admitting that she planned on going back to being a barista and saving up for online classes didn't seem like the right answer. Suddenly, she realized that those were dreams of a different Lyla, one that didn't know what it was like to be birdnapped and experimented on. Being fully recovered and able to leave WANC seemed months away from where she was now. And while she yearned to be home, the thought of moving back in with her family wasn't entirely what she wanted. While she loved her younger siblings, at times the nest felt a little crowded. Lyla was ready to start her own life.

As if noticing the uncertainty in her mind, Lee went on as if this was a rehearsed conversation. "ASS has its training facilities in Australia if you're looking for a change of pace."

A change. Lyla could use a change. But could she leave all her siblings behind? Or her job at the coffee shop—if her position was still open? There's no way it was. Lyla had been missing for half a year prior to coming to WANC for rehab. Maybe she could find a different coffee shop to work at. But what if she wasn't able to blend in with regular humans again? Did ASS have a tech division? Lyla did love computers, after all. The thought of leaving was enticing. Spreading her wings and finding her own nest. A bout of homesickness struck as soon as she had the thought. "I don't know if I'm ready for that yet."

"Think about what it might do to help your recovery, then. Do you think you'd rather be somewhere with more birds—"

"Agent Lee!" The new voice sent a shiver down Lyla's spine, even though it wasn't directed at her. She turned her head to see Clarice Tertius, legendary hawk shifter, heading in their direction. Lyla couldn't believe Clarice was in the same building as her! She'd heard so many stories about the shifter that she felt in the presence of a famous person. Albeit a crabby one.

"Shit," Agent Lee hissed before standing. "Agent Tertius. How nice to see you." Agent Lee's tone implied the opposite.

"I wish I could say the same," the former ASS agent spat, narrowing her eyes at the current ASS agent. "How many times do I need to remind you that the aviary is off-limits? No trying to poach FUCN'A patients. They're here for recovery, not for ASS recruitment."

"Tell that to our boss." Lee shrugged.

"*Your* boss," Tertius retorted, wrinkling her nose in disgust. "You ASSes can try to claim me all you want, but I'm fully FUC."

Lee ignored the statement. "You know ASS is pissed about this new aviary. They think FUC is trying to expand into ASS territory." Lee raised her head defiantly, showing she agreed with this perspective.

"They can be as pissed as they want about it," Tertius replied. "But just as FUC is going to stand their ground and refuse to ship off a bunch of rescued patients—ripping them away from what family and support groups they have here— they're also damn well going to approve building structures that will enhance the patients' quality of life. Regardless of how insecure that might make a bunch of ASSes." A wry smile spread across her face as if she were proud of her pun.

"And I can respect that. But you have to admit there are a lot of birds here now."

"Blame that on the slew of illegal experimenters who think the Rocky Mountains are a great place to hide their labs. If your bosses don't want FUC to help the rescued patients, then they're welcome to establish something in the neighborhood so they can take in whatever bird comes our way."

"Most ASS agents hate the Canadian cold," Lee muttered, making Lyla wonder if she was one of them. Lyla was aware that there were many ASS agents who worked for FUC "on loan," even more now that Sandy's lab was busted up and so many birds were now at FUCN'A recovering. "Anyway, Lyla, it was nice to meet you. Please search me out if you have any questions." She set an ASS business card with her contact information on the tray next to Lyla. "Clarice... I wish I could say it was nice seeing you again." With that, Agent Lee left.

"There's no pressure for you to decide what to do once you're released," Agent Tertius reassured Lyla, taking the seat Agent Lee had vacated. "There's no rush on your recovery, either."

"Okay." Lyla wasn't sure what to say. Clarice had an imposing presence and felt almost like a celebrity.

"Is there anything you need? Anything that could make things better for you?" Clarice asked, sounding genuinely concerned.

Lyla couldn't help herself. She blurted out, "Could I take a trip to the library?"

"The library?" Clarice raised an eyebrow.

"I wish I had my smartphone, but, well, bad guys don't let you keep it after capture, and my mom hasn't been able to afford to buy me a new one." It wasn't all that important, usually, except now she wanted to help her new friend.

"Sure. I don't see a problem with it. As long as you don't spend too much time away and you're back in the hospital wing before that IV bag is empty."

Lyla's heart soared. She thanked Clarice and stood, having finished her tray of snacks. Dr. Brown and the nurses didn't pay her any attention as she left the aviary, but Lyla couldn't shake the feeling that she was doing something against the rules, even if she had permission.

Permission from someone who's not on my medical team, she thought as she followed the signs to the academic wing. There, she found a placard with the locations of classrooms, staff offices, and… the library with a computer lab.

Excitement buzzed in her chest, like the flutter of hummingbird wings, like her own wings. Dr. Brown said soon she wouldn't need the glucose drip and she'd be able to get all the nutrients she needed from food, as she once could. They didn't want to risk Lyla shifting before they gave her permission to. In hummingbird form, she blew through a lot of calories per second. She didn't want to risk it either. Then she'd be stuck on the dextrose drip even longer. Though she and her IV bag had become close, she didn't want him around forever. She wanted a real friend. And Lyla hoped going to the computer lab to conduct research would help her with just that.

5

———————

Gabby began to say her goodbyes to her mom and Phin before she turned to leave. Her mom's soft fingertips pressed into her arm, holding her back. "I have something for you," she said, the whisper of a smile on her visage.

Phin unburied his face from Kristen's other arm, brushing the long hair out of his bright blue eyes, rimmed with red from crying. Gabby's heart broke. It shattered into a million pieces, like a glass vase on a marble floor. How many more times could she endure that expression on her brother's face? She clenched her fist around the crow Phin had given her. She relaxed her hand, not wanting to accidentally break the gift. It was really considerate. And Phin would be crushed if anything happened to it. She pictured him doing extra chores around the house to afford not one but two figurines. And the thought he put into it. *Dad can keep it in his beak when he changes back into a crow.* Would she have been as attentive at Phin's age? She didn't think so. For ten years, Gabby had been an only child before Phin was born. The world used to revolve around her, at least her parents' world.

Now she wanted anything more than being the center of attention.

Kristen opened the bag on the couch, pulling out two thin books. "One's a crossword puzzle and the other a word search. I thought it could be fun practice. Lynn said she gives you similar homework." It was the consoling voice of her childhood, the one she heard after a scraped knee or a nightmare. It offered protection, patience, and love. The best ingredients to heal.

Gabby shook her head before nodding. Instead of getting frustrated with herself, she sung the word, "Yes," on a random note.

Her mom raised an eyebrow, probably fearing something else had gone wrong with Gabby's brain. She shrugged. "It helps. Lynn had me try it today," she sang with oscillating notes. Crows weren't known for their beautiful singing, but at least she wasn't off-key. Maybe her new friend Lyla was better at singing and could help her out in the tune department. Her heart fluttered at the thought of spending more time with her.

"Cool!" Phin hopped off the couch, his sadness seemingly forgotten. "You can pretend you're in a musical and sing all day." His bright smile and hopefulness patched up some of Gabby's broken heart. A little bit anyway.

Gabby took the books from her mother's hands. "Th-th…" She squeezed her eyes tight, really focusing on what she wanted to say, picturing it in a song. "Thank you," she sang. Kristen and Phin hugged her tight. Phin beamed at her before turning away, Kristen placing a reassuring arm around his shoulder. Gabby watched the pair disappear around the corner at the end of the hall.

Gabby walked back to her room, clutching the books to her chest, the tiny bird still wrapped in her fingers. She glanced at the poster promoting Huggie's party next to the nurses' station. She considered ripping it off the wall. Then a crazy thought popped into her head. What if her new friend planned to go? It might not be so bad to attend, in that case, considering Lyla seemed more than content to do all the talking. Besides, the woman was beautiful and kind.

Butterflies formed in Gabby's stomach at the thought of asking Lyla out. What if she said no? Wait. What if Gabby couldn't even ask? She bit her lip. Maybe she could mime it to her like a round of charades. She chuckled at the mental image of her trying to act it out and Lyla guessing all the wrong things. She was never very good at the game.

She popped her head into room 102—the room Lyla had said was hers. A messy bed and an empty tray of food sat in the center of the room. A large bouquet of flowers fanned out near the windows. A quick pang of jealousy nipped at Gabby. It stifled the second she noticed the *Get well. Love, Mom* scrawled on the card in fancy cursive sticking out of the wrapper. She felt guilty for the brief tang of jealousy, though she couldn't help it. She glanced to the open door of the empty bathroom. Her pink-haired friend was nowhere to be seen. While Gabby wasn't ready to ask her out, she'd hoped to see a friendly face. Maybe she was remembering the room number wrong. She didn't think so. It wasn't unusual for patients to not be in their rooms. Many had a slew of doctor and therapy appointments.

Her heart sank a little while staring at the vacant bed. Maybe Lyla was discharged. While that would be great news for Lyla, Gabby felt lonely after the thought. She'd started looking forward to having a new friend, someone who wasn't family, someone without expectations who knew what she was going through. The staff seemed to understand, but they were her caretakers, not her friends. Dad got it, but between the both of them, they could hardly get through a conversation. Lyla seemed happy to chat on by herself, putting no pressure on Gabby to talk much. That made it less stressful.

Then Gabby noticed some items on the table next to the bed. Her heart lifted. *She can't be discharged, not if her things are still here!* The picture was of Lyla—sans feathers—standing next to four boys of various ages. *They must be her family.* A small pebble sat next to the frame. Gabby stared at it, wondering what its significance was. A good luck charm maybe.

She thought back to the crown of feathers around Lyla's head. Some of the rescued experiments started out human, but others had been born shifters. Was Lyla always a hummingbird shifter, or was this world new to her? They didn't talk about that last night, but Gabby didn't think Lyla started out human. Sandy seemed to favor birds. Dr. Grimm did, too. Nausea roiled in Gabby's stomach at the thought of the bad doctor. He had to be at-large still. Not that she was able to inquire about it—though not for lack of trying—but she got the feeling he was lurking about, biding his time. But for what? She didn't want to know. It would be wonderful if she never saw that creep again.

Gabby left Lyla's room and walked on down the hallway, nodding her greetings to the doctors and nurses that filled the space. Most of them made their rounds and checked on patients. Some traveled to the breakroom for a much-needed caffeine fix.

Her room seemed too far away. Gabby didn't have the mental fortitude to try to converse with anyone. She clutched her new presents to her chest, powerwalking down the hall to avoid speaking to any chatty staff or patients. Her spirits rose slightly when she made it to her room. Trying to talk earlier had been tiring. Seeing her family was exhausting. And not their fault in any way. *It is what it is.* It was just hard.

The summer sun must have been on vacation. The cloudy sky ushered in rain that streaked down the window. It left a small puddle on the sill. *Odd.* Gabby couldn't recall leaving the window open. Maybe one of the nurses decided she needed fresh air and opened it. They were always trying to convince her to sit outside in one of the courtyards.

"Being inside all the time isn't going to help you heal," Nurse Mya would remind her. Gabby knew the nurse meant well but figured she'd speak the same whether she was inside or out.

She set down her gifts on the table next to the bed and crossed the room to the window. She toed the wet tiles, not wanting to soak the slippers she wore. Nothing pissed her off more than a wet foot. She doubted even aquatic shifters enjoyed that experience.

She slid the window shut, noticing the screen was torn as the gentle breeze blew in. *Odd.* She didn't remember it being like that before. She'd have to let someone know. She looked to the mess of water on the sill and the floor, shuddering at the thought of having to ask someone for a towel. They'd probably want to know why she needed one. That would be too many words.

As she surveyed the mess, she noticed a slip of paper peeking out from under the wall-mounted heater/air conditioner unit. Gabby hoped it wasn't important because it seemed to have absorbed a good deal of water. She carefully extracted it before unfolding it, wary that wet paper tore easily.

Gabby couldn't make sense of what she saw. It appeared to be a map of WANC, detailing the various spaces inside, including the hospital wing. Last Gabby knew, they weren't giving maps out to visitors, and staff wouldn't need one, so who did this belong to?

Gabby jumped as a staff member, Char, entered the room, tray in hand.

"It's lunchtime," they announced, placing the tray on the side table that could roll over to cross the bed. Char's brows raised after noting the look on Gabby's face. "I swear they didn't accidentally give you chicken noodle soup again. It's tomato. See?" They pointed to the thick orange liquid in the bowl next to the grilled cheese sandwich. Even though the kitchen used certified shifter-free meat, and wild crows might eat nestling birds, Gabby chose to not eat birds on principle. It felt wrong, though other types of meat were just fine.

Gabby shook her head and held out the saturated paper. "Found." She breathed deep and focused, trying to find that part of her brain that was used in singing. Picturing herself singing the words, she sang-talked, "I found this by the window."

Char's eyes widened. "Oh my gosh, Gabby. That was a full sentence!"

A hot blush filled Gabby's cheeks. She hated being the center of attention, even if there were only two people in the room. She especially didn't know how to take compliments. Instead of trying to muddle through saying thanks, she pointed at the window, bringing Char back to the problem at hand. "Right." Char glanced down at the paper, careful not to rip it. Their dark brows wrinkled up in interest. "This is a map of the hospital." Concern replaced the joy on Char's face. "Show me exactly where you found this."

Gabby crouched down, pointing to the place on the floor where she found the map. Then she stood, opening the window and flicking the torn screen. She had enough talking for one day and felt Char could piece together what she was implying.

Char poked their fingers through the hole in the screen.

"That's large enough for a small shifter, wouldn't you say?" Char locked their deep green eyes on Gabby, anxiety printed on their face.

Gabby nodded. Though she shouldn't have felt relief, she did. It came in quick waves, washing away the worry from before, if only because now she wasn't alone in this. Char would help her.

But it brought a new reason for anxiety. If the paper wasn't dropped from someone inside WANC, that meant someone who shouldn't be there now was. Gabby felt her eyes widen as she locked eyes with Char, the meaning of what they implied sinking in. She immediately thought to Dr. Grimm. He was back. And that meant she wasn't safe.

And she still couldn't get the words out to explain it.

6

Lyla followed the signs to the library. The few cadets and FUC agents she passed paid her little mind. One cadet asked which instructor's class was so challenging that she needed an IV bag to recover. She wasn't sure why she felt self-conscious about admitting she was one of the rescued experiments. Usually that was pretty apparent with the feathers sticking out of her head—in the hospital wing at any rate. Instead of explaining her situation, she spit out, "Agent Stone." She said the name of the only FUC agent she knew—which was only because he'd been the agent working her case. Lyla hoped he was an instructor too. *Feathers crossed.* With any luck, it was a good guess.

The cadet seemed satisfied. "I heard he's tough. I hope you at least got a good grade," the cadet added before leaving Lyla to her mission.

The doors to the library proved not hard to find. Lyla expected some attention with the IV bag in tow, but everyone she passed seemed to think it was as normal as Maude's meatless meatballs. Rolling the stand with the IV bag across the transition strip on the floor separating the library from the hall was a struggle she had not anticipated. The metal clanged and the tiny wheels rattled before she gave up and carried the stand over the threshold.

The librarian—Albert according to the nameplate across his desk—narrowed his eyes at her before putting his finger to his lips in a shushing gesture. She felt herself shrink slightly in embarrassment. "Sorry." Once satisfied she was warned and would be quiet, he went back to the stack of books before him.

She glanced around, hoping to see a row of computers. Afraid to ask the librarian she'd already managed to piss off before fully setting foot inside the library, Lyla decided to wander around and not ask for directions. Besides, she had nothing but time on her hands. After meandering through and around various stacks and shelves of books, she found some desks with computers.

"I told you we'd find it," she whispered to the bag, afraid to draw the unwanted attention of Albert by talking too loudly. She sat at one of the terminals, hoping you didn't need a password to log on. The computer came alive after she shook the mouse. Maybe with the number of guests around WANC, like the rehab patients, they didn't see the need for passwords and wanted everyone to feel as at home as possible. Whatever the reason, she was thankful.

Lyla's fingers flew across the keyboard. Without her smartphone, she was jonesing for technology. She loved computers and video games. The common area where the video game console was located always seemed to be monopolized by a flock of seagull shifters. If the hospital wing took comment cards, she'd leave one saying more entertainment was needed. Some of the patients required a lot of time for rehab. It seemed to her that the baddies who experimented on them had no idea how they got the results they did. That made it challenging for the doctors at WANC to reverse it.

Plus, the apprehended sickos who experimented on them didn't like to give up the secrets they did have. It made the healing process that much more difficult.

A slew of websites on Broca's aphasia opened up, and she dug in, reading various articles about the affliction Gabby had. She learned that, with it, both writing and speaking were difficult. It seemed there were no shortcuts to improving. Patients needed intensive therapy to relearn how to speak.

Disappointed that there didn't seem to be a magic cure for her new friend, Lyla kept reading, focusing on the things that those around the patients could do to help. Keeping them company was one thing—people in isolation healed slower than those surrounded by friends and family. Lyla also read that helping Gabby to finish her sentences by giving her the next letter or sound could be helpful, but that seemed more like a practice thing. If Lyla didn't know what Gabby was trying to say, she wouldn't be able to help her out. Unless it was a word she was already asking her to say.

Lyla frowned at the current article on her screen. It helped a little, she supposed. She was looking more for a miracle. Something that could completely put her friend at ease. Something impossible. Healing was difficult, she knew that and tried to forget it most days.

She looked to the clock on the wall. The hour hand was creeping close to noon. Her eyes moved to her IV bag. It was getting low and would need to be changed soon, and she didn't want to get in trouble for letting it run out. It was time to leave.

Lyla got up from the computer feeling less hopeful than she had upon entering the library. At least she learned a bit about the condition. That was more than she knew this morning. And it had gotten her out of her room. If she stared at those four walls any longer, she'd be the one screaming into her pillow tonight. She thought about Huggie's party. It was something to look forward to. But would Gabby go if she asked her?

She grabbed the bar of the IV tower and shepherded it along next to her. Careful not to piss off Albert and risk making too much noise, Lyla glided the wheels of the device across the library floor. They rattled softly. She flicked her gaze to Albert. He'd buried his nose in another stack of books. In fact, he barely seemed to notice she was leaving. She'd toed the threshold of the door back into the hallway when the shifter piped up, "Cadet?"

Lyla turned on her heel, her heart hammered in her ears. "Y-yes?" she asked, hoping a hole would open in the floor and swallow her. It would save her from talking her way out of whatever predicament she found herself in. She was quieter than a mouse shifter. *What could I have possibly done to attract his attention?* Lyla feared that if she got in trouble, she'd never be able to visit the library—or the computers—again.

"I hope to see you around here more when you're feeling better. It's always good to see a new face."

Lyla smiled. She could tell he genuinely meant it. "I will." She looked back at the computers. Her hands were at home on the keys and controlling the mouse. It felt as normal as the outfit she now wore. "I really miss my computer," she added. After giving Albert her thanks, she headed off.

She plucked the IV stand from the floor and plopped it onto the tiles on the other side. After letting out a sigh of relief that she managed to not make a lot of noise this time, she inspected the hallway for anyone who looked nosy or like hospital staff. That last thing she wanted was to be lectured about letting her drip get too low. She was about to wander on when she caught the glimpse of a thick, pink worm flicking around the corner at the end of the hallway. Lyla rubbed at her eyes. They must have been playing tricks on her. Why would there be a large worm in the hallway?

Instead of walking toward the hospital wing, she wheeled her IV bag after the mysterious creature, but it was quicker than she expected, and by the time she made it to its location, it was gone. She rubbed at her head, feeling confused. Was her sugar too low and she was hallucinating? She didn't think so. The dextrose drip was low but not yet empty.

"I guess in a place full of shifters, what can you expect?" she asked her IV bag with a shrug. The mystery of the worm could have to wait for another day. Lyla shuffled down the hall. The excitement of her adventure had worn her out. She turned the corner, following the sign back to the hospital wing of WANC, still thinking about the worm, or whatever creature she saw scuttle around the corner at the opposite end of the hall. Small shifters shouldn't wander around inside the building in their shifter forms—they risked getting stepped on!

She must've been delusional after exerting herself. At least that was what Lyla told herself to keep the nagging feeling that someone who wasn't supposed to be at FUCN'A was there.

"It's just my anxiety blowing things out of proportion," she reminded the IV bag as it rolled along beside her. "Now, let's get back to our room and get you changed out. After a little nap, we can see if Gabby is up for a visit."

7

———

Char rushed Gabby out of her room with the soggy map. They marched up to the nurses' station, grabbing one of the phones from the desk. Char's well-manicured nails punched a few numbers. "Butters, no! I am not the pizza delivery person." Char rolled their eyes and sighed. "This is Char, in the hospital wing. I need security. We have evidence that there may be an intruder in the building." After Char hung up the phone, they turned to Gabby. "Sorry about that. They're always thinking with their stomachs. They're goat shifters. They'll eat anything."

Char dropped the dripping handwritten map onto the counter before rubbing their hands on their scrubs. "Take a seat. I know you're shaken up."

Gabby shook her head. She couldn't sit. Couldn't try to relax. Not until security arrived and took care of things.

The minutes it took for security to arrive felt like hours. Gabby's stomach was doing summersaults. She wanted this over as quickly as possible.

Finally, a man and woman in grey security uniforms sidled up to the nurses' station. The woman popped some potato chips from the bag she was carrying into her mouth while the man stared at Gabby. "Is this the intruder?" His blue eyes scanned her as he made for the handcuffs on his belt.

"No..." Char answered. "I said we have evidence of a possible intruder."

"Is she the evidence?" the woman guard asked between crunches on the chips, nodding toward Gabby.

Gabby supposed she kind of was. At least she was witness to the evidence. She pointed to the soggy paper on the counter. "Map. On floor."

The male guard picked it up and sniffed. "It doesn't smell edible."

Char rolled her eyes. "I don't think it's supposed to be. Either way, don't eat the evidence."

"We unfortunately don't handle evidence. You'll want to get an agent up here for that. But we can search for the intruder." Her curly brown hair jiggled as she shook her head. She grabbed a granola bar from her pocket and peeled the wrapper back before taking a bite. "Where do you think the intruder entered?" she asked after swallowing the last bite. Gabby wondered how someone who ate so much could be so skinny. The guard was rail thin.

"My... room... 106," Gabby answered, rattling off her room number and pointing down the hall.

The male guard nodded. "I'll radio FUC to send a hound shifter to sniff out the trail and ask the rest of the security team to review the cameras." He turned to his companion. "Let's check the room then complete a sweep of the building. We'll break for pizza then check the perimeter." The woman nodded, and both guards sauntered down the hallway.

Gabby looked to Char, whose shoulders deflated after a long sigh. "I hoped they'd be able to do more or somehow already know who the intruder was," Char said with a shrug.

Char seemed just as shaken up about the intruder as Gabby was.

Gabby shook her head. She was trying to find the words to reassure Char when Agent Stone waltzed up in his cowboy boots.

"Did someone request a hound shifter to track a scent?" His brown eyes twinkled with delight. Agent Stone clearly enjoyed tracking scents. What Basset Hound shifter wouldn't?

Gabby was instantly relieved to see him. Agent Stone was all Phin talked about for months following their rescue. Apparently, Phin had known that Gabby and their dad were kept below the old abandoned mall near their dad's house. He hung out there for hours, trying to launch his own investigation, until Agent Sparks and Stone's own investigation eventually brought them to the same mall. Together, the three of them found the secret entrance to the evil lair of Sandy, and they were able to rescue all the trapped shifters.

Agent Stone had taken care of business then, and Gabby was sure he'd do the same now.

Char filled him in. "The window to Gabby's room was open, and there was a tear in the screen. She found this map." Char handed Agent Stone the wet paper.

He rubbed at the stubble forming on his chin as he assessed the situation. Then Agent Stone crossed his arms across his flannel shirt. "Any idea as to who could have been in your room?"

Just the thought of Dr. Grimm tangled Gabby's brain. A cold sweat dripped icy fingers down her spine at the memory of his thin voice in her ear. "G-g-Grimm. Back. F-f-favorite." She stomped her foot in frustration. No helpful words were coming out of her mouth.

Agent Stone put a reassuring hand on Gabby's shoulder. "It's okay. We'll try to find whoever it was."

"Grimm. Grimm…" She balled her fists in anger.

"Don't worry." Agent Stone's voice was calm, soothing. But it wasn't enough to squelch Gabby's frustration. Why did she always get so tongue-tied when trying to talk about Dr. Grimm? True, the man scared her half to death, but still. "Where did the security guards go?"

"My room." *Of course I got that out.* Gabby crossed her arms.

"If there's anyone after you, we'll find them," Agent Stone reassured her, as if reading her worries. "I'm one of the best trackers at FUC. If there's a scent, I can follow it."

Gabby thought about the puddle of water on the floor. She didn't know much about scents or tracking, but didn't water somehow wash it away? She sighed. She was all the help she could have been. And of course, the one thing she couldn't do? Explain her theory that Dr. Grimm was behind this. He was probably searching for his former experiments to finish his evil agenda. Alas, as far as Agent Stone knew, Dr. Grimm didn't exist, and Gabby couldn't form the words to change that fact.

Gabby couldn't stop thinking of the terrible things Dr. Grimm had whispered in her ear. *You're my favorite.* A cold bead of sweat trickled down her spine. She grabbed Agent Stone's shirtsleeve, trying to get it all out before he left. As capable as he was, what if he couldn't put the pieces together and Dr. Grimm snatched her up again? She stuttered and stammered until Agent Stone offered her a gentle smile.

"Lynn is out of the office today, but I'll come back tomorrow and maybe the three of us together can work on this some more. Would you like to change rooms? It may ease your mind while we're working to find the intruder." His suggestion soothed her raw nerves.

Gabby nodded. That could work. If the intruder recognized that as her room, moving would keep them guessing.

She'd have to make sure to let Lyla know she moved. She couldn't bear the thoughts of Lyla thinking she'd left without saying goodbye.

Agent Stone turned to one of the nurses at the station who was just signing off her computer to complete another set of rounds. "How quickly can a new room be made available for Gabby?" Agent Stone asked, the worry clear in his voice.

"Let me see." The nurse logged back onto the computer. Her brows wrinkled as she clicked the mouse. "We're actually cleaning a room on the other side of the hall, room 118. It should be ready within the hour. I'll make a note Gabby's moving."

"Thank you." Agent Stone turned back to Gabby and Char. "Keep your eyes peeled for anything suspicious. Gabby, work on gathering your things. I'll check in with security to see if they found anything on the tapes after I see if I can find a scent. I'm the best tracker there is, Gabby. If there's a scent, I'll be able to follow it."

Gabby smiled to say thanks.

Char squeezed her shoulder. "If there's anything to find, they'll track it down." And with that, they left for the kitchens.

Just as Agent Stone left for Gabby's room, Lyla appeared. Lyla smiled when the FUC agent nodded in greeting and kept on moving. "What's wrong?" Lyla sked, leaning against the edge of the counter of the nurses' station like it was the tip of a branch. Her voice was as soft as the down of a baby bird. She must have been able to tell by the expression on Gabby's face that she was stressed to the max.

She looked up to Lyla, her eyes wide. Patience and understanding filled Lyla's heart-shaped face. A pale rose color filled her full lips. Gabby wondered how sweet Lyla would taste. Suddenly, she realized she was staring at her, and embarrassment flooded her.

She leaned forward, letting her long hair hide the blush blossoming on her cheeks. The heat from it snaked up her neck, pooling into her face. *Where is my trusty pillow?* The temptation to hide under it was strong, but she had to focus. She gulped down the cool air, concentrating on the words she wanted to say. One at a time, tasting them in her mouth before trying them out.

"Come. Please. Help." Lyla blanched, so Gabby tried to explain, "Moving rooms."

"Oh, okay." Gabby appreciated Lyla's patience and the fact that she didn't push for more answers, only followed her down the hall.

They neared Gabby's room as the security guards were just leaving. One of the guards was holding a pile of clothes, the other a pair of cowboy boots that Agent Stone had been wearing. "The room's clear, ma'am," the male guard said.

Agent Stone—in hound form—soon followed, his long, brown floppy ears swaying as he sauntered down the hall, nose nearly stuck to the ground.

After the trio were halfway down the hall, Lyla gently touched Gabby's arm. "Did something happen?" Her eyes were wide with worry.

"A map. Found a map." Gabby entered her room and pointed to the dried-up spot on the floor where the puddle from the window had soaked the floor earlier.

"A map of what? WANC?"

Gabby closed her eyes and focused. She nodded her head. "Think they outsider."

Lyla's hazel eyes widened, the afternoon sun illuminating the green flecks in the brown, emeralds strewn across a dark, sandy beach. "You mean an unwanted visitor dropped this after breaking into WANC? In your room?"

"Visiting family. Happened when."

"You think it happened when you were visiting your family?" Her brows wrinkled in concern as her eyes widened.

Gabby looked to the window and the hole in the screen. Lyla followed the invisible trail her gaze left. She got up, crossing the room. After leaning forward to inspect the scene of the crime, she popped up. "There's a tear in the screen," Lyla observed, her voice slightly higher in pitch than normal. Gabby nodded to let her know she knew. "So Agent Stone saw this?' Gabby continued to nod. It seemed the repetition was helping her to continue the gesture.

Lyla came back to the bed and sat down, running her fingers through her messy hair. Even with the feathers, her hair seemed more unkempt than yesterday. As if noticing Gabby's gaze, Lyla explained, "I might have overdone it this morning."

"Need time. To heal." Gabby tried to remind her friend not to move so fast. She figured that, as a hummingbird shifter, Lyla would need all the reminders she could get.

"I know I know. I probably shouldn't have." Lyla tossed her hands up. "I just get so sick of being cooped up, you know? They say I have to rest and keep building up my energy, but I can't keep sitting in my room. So after we had some shifting practice, I asked if I could go to the computer lab." She hung her head.

Computers. She wore herself out playing on computers? Gabby raised an eyebrow.

Lyla glanced up, noting Gabby's expression. "Don't look at me like that," Lyla joked with a lighthearted chuckle. "I love computers. But I was hoping to find something that would help me help you talk. I know that sounds stupid." The words tumbled out of her mouth in an avalanche of syllables. "Like I thought I could fix something the doctors and nurses and therapists here couldn't. But I just thought..." She leaned back and sighed, shaking her head. "I don't know what I thought. I just wanted to help." She dropped her hands in her lap.

Gabby reached forward and put a hand on Lyla's. Lyla didn't pull away. She glanced up at her, smiling. That gave Gabby an idea. She pulled out the books her mom bought her. "This helps."

Lyla looked to the books. Her face lit up. "That's one of the things I read about." She clasped her hands together in excitement. "Maybe we can work on a puzzle together after you move rooms." She flicked her eyes to Gabby, waiting for her response.

Gabby hadn't considered that it was a thing she could do with others. The books seemed like a solitary thing—a lonely thing—for her to practice. Something to pass the time when she wasn't in an appointment or screaming into her pillow. An activity that bordered on the idea of fun but could never be fun since they were all word puzzles and Gabby struggled with language. But to have someone helping, or even just sitting nearby for company, that did sound enjoyable.

"What's that?" Lyla pointed to the toy crow Phin had given Gabby earlier.

"Present from brother." Gabby paused in between each word, concentration honing her mind. Her words were finally starting to come together, but everything seemed easier somehow with Lyla around. "Crow shifter." She pointed to herself.

Lyla beamed up at her. "What a thoughtful gift. You're a crow shifter, so he bought you a toy crow." She eyed the present, her face glowing with happiness. Lyla had such a warm personality that it was infectious. Gabby caught a smile forming on her face. Lyla was her hope.

And maybe with the help of the word games, she'd be able to finally talk about what had been on her mind: Dr. Grimm.

"Where are you moving to?" Lyla's tone sounded chipper, though her dark hazel eyes seemed troubled.

"One eighteen." Gabby glanced at her sparse belongings. At least she had someone to help. Though if she didn't have a friend, she was sure one of the staff members would have assisted her.

"Let's get stared then." Lyla beamed a toothy smile at her, the remnants of concern leaving her eyes.

Before Gabby picked up her pile of word puzzle books, she glanced back to the hole in the screen. With an intruder on campus, she'd have to be careful. Despite campus security and Agent Stone, looking for said intruder, thinking it was random, Gabby was certain this was linked to her case. There was no doubt in her mind it had something to do with the evil doctor who'd held her captive. And if the map was, in fact, connected to him, it was only a matter of time before he'd come looking for her. If the intruder started in her room and was attempting to capture her, why had they left? They could've sat in wait somewhere out of sight in her room. And by the look of the tiny slash in the screen, the creature could have easily hidden anywhere. So why had it wandered off?

8

———

Lyla watched the shadow of worry cross her friend's face. Gabby flicked her gaze from the books in her lap to the window and then back. "Penny for your thoughts?" Lyla wanted to know if there was anything else she could do to help. Changing rooms didn't appear to be the only thing on Gabby's mind. And who could blame her? Someone had broken into her room. At least Gabby wasn't there when it happened. Lyla was thankful for that. She didn't want to think about anyone kidnapping her friend. She wanted to protect her from going through anything like that again.

Gabby brushed her long, wavy hair behind her shoulders, exposing the growing look of concern. She sighed, looking up at the ceiling, probably to find her words. Concentration etched deep lines in her pretty face. "D-doctor Grimm." Her lips puckered as if tasting something sour and repulsive.

"Doctor who?" Lyla had never heard the name before.

"Grimm. Looking. For. Me." The phrase seemed to take all of Gabby's energy, but a look of triumph, with a smile, flashed across her face.

"Was he at the lab with Sandy?" Lyla couldn't recall a Dr.

Grimm at her lab, though she was kept in a different location from where Gabby was being held—if Gabby's chart was correct. How the baddies were funding all these labs, Lyla didn't know. But there seemed to be a lot of them.

Gabby paused before nodding her head. Normally Lyla would take a hesitation to mean the other person was hiding something, but in this instance, she knew it took a lot of time for Gabby to focus on what she wanted to say, for it to come out in the correct order and with the correct words or gestures.

Lyla rubbed her chin. "Why do you think he's looking for you? Because the map was in your room?"

This time, Gabby shook her head. Lyla was about to ask if she meant to nod when Gabby tried to explain. "Said… was… favorite… his." Long pauses punctuated each word, but Lyla waited until Gabby finished to piece it together.

"He said you were his favorite?" Gabby nodded to confirm Lyla translated correctly. "That's ominous."

Gabby sighed, leaning back against the wall behind her.

"That's… That's really shitty." Lyla didn't know what else to say. It wasn't often that she found herself at a loss for words.

The memory of the worm flopping around the corner in the hall popped into her mind. Was that somehow connected? "I need to tell you something."

"What?"

"Remember when I told you I was at the library?"

"Nnyes…" The two words blended together in a long, drawn-out mix of both.

"Look how good you're getting! You corrected yourself mid-word. And you haven't confused your nods or head shakes since I've seen you today." A bright happiness blossomed inside of Lyla. Her six months in hell had been rough, and the healing afterward wasn't much better, but watching Gabby improve seemingly overnight was priceless.

"Focus." Gabby seemed to have other things on her mind than her progress. Lyla could understand why. Someone might be here to recapture her.

"Right. I was leaving the library when I thought I saw a worm flop around the corner at the end of the hall. It was so weird to see that I convinced myself I was having a low-sugar hallucination." The works tumbled out. The fast speech was a sign her energy reserves were filling up and almost back to normal.

"Flop?" Gabby raised an eyebrow in curiosity. "Worm?"

Though neither word formed a complete sentence, Lyla thought she understood the meaning well enough based off of Gabby's tone. "Worms don't usually flop, do they?" Gabby shook her head. "What the hell do you think it was?"

This time Gabby shrugged her shoulders. "Need. Tell Stone. Or security."

Lyla took that to mean Gabby agreed that she needed to tell Agent Stone or campus security what she saw. It could be nothing, but it could mean the safety of Gabby—or others. Lyla briefly met Agent Stone when she first was rescued. He seemed nice enough. But he seemed kind of busy tracking. Maybe security could track the worm—or whatever it was— on the cameras.

"You coming?" Lyla asked Gabby as she stood up to leave and headed to the door, rolling her IV bag behind her. "We can't let Dr. Grimm get you."

Gabby looked cautiously at the door and bit her lip. Lyla could tell that the idea of leaving her room was unnerving.

"I'll be right by your side," she promised. "And I'll do all the talking."

Hesitantly, Gabby stood. "Okay."

Lyla smiled. She led the way, feeling like she would have

skipped if her cautious friend hadn't been walking so slowly. She offered her hand to hold, and Gabby took it, lacing her fingers thorough hers. The nurses and doctors buzzed about down the hallway, weaving in and out of rooms. Some wore scrubs, others white lab coats; all of them looked busy. Not wanting to bother them, Lyla stopped at the nearest nurses' station, where a man with red, curly hair stopped his typing on the computer long enough to glance up at Lyla.

"Can I help you?" The smile he offered didn't quite reach his eyes, and Lyla could see he was stressed but still trying to be pleasant.

"Do you know if Agent Stone or the security guards are still around?"

"I haven't seen them in a little bit. Sorry."

Lyla did her best not to be disappointed or impatient. She couldn't imagine the stress of working here. Though, in her opinion, it was far more stressful to be one of the patients. "Can we go find them?"

The nurse shook his head. "No one is allowed to leave the hospital wing without permission."

Lyla bit her lip in a mix of frustration and worry. "But it's really important."

He sighed. "Even if you had permission to wander the campus, there's no telling where Agent Stone is. He was hot on the trail of a scent when he walked past. The best I can do is send an email for you and he'll get back to you when he can. I think all of security is doing a sweep of the perimeter."

"Can't wait." Gabby spoke up, to Lyla's surprise. She turned away from the nurse to look at her friend, who had a look of determination she'd yet to see on her face.

Lyla turned back to the nurse to elaborate. "Gabby and I have something important to tell them. It's about the same thing Gabby has talked to Agent Stone about—the break-in to her room. I think." She glanced behind her at Gabby, and Gabby nodded.

"Okay, all right, one sec." The nurse picked up his phone, looking at his computer screen before punching in an extension. After a few moments, he hung up and tried another set of numbers. After another minute, he put the receiver back in its cradle. "Agent Stone didn't answer his office phone, and the directory doesn't have his cell phone. I can send an email to let him know you need to talk to him urgently. I can message security as well. They didn't answer there when I called either. They must be still out of the office checking the perimeter and left their walkie-talkies on the charger... again."

"What about ASS Agent Sparks? She was working my case." She briefly met the fiery ASS agent once and immediately liked her.

He clicked around on his computer. "She's not in the directory. Is she on staff here?"

"Oh." Lyla felt herself deflate. "No, I guess she's not." She blushed, remembering they were at a FUC facility and Agent Sparks worked for ASS. How could she forget such a detail after her run-in with Agent Lee earlier?

The nurse nodded sympathetically. "I'll mention in the email that you're looking for her too. Maybe Agent Stone knows how to get ahold of her. There, I just sent it. They'll be down to talk to you when they can."

"But—"

"I understand that this is important to you two, but that's the best I can do for now while they are busy. As soon as they're free, they'll touch base with you." The nurse's eyes softened with understanding.

Lyla bit her lip, holding back additional sass. The nurse was right. Even if it felt like an emergency to them, it didn't mean they had immediate access to the agents.

"Are either of you in immediate trouble? I can page security to come up and talk to you now. One of them will have to briefly stop their check of the perimeter though."

"No," Gabby piped up again. "Stone. Please."

The nurse nodded.

Lyla looked back at Gabby. "Are you sure?"

"Yes." She said it with enough certainty that Lyla didn't argue.

"All right, thank you," Lyla said dejectedly to the nurse, turning away from the station. She felt somewhat comforted when Gabby patted her shoulder, until a scream pierced the buzzing of the hospital wing.

"What's going on?" she asked as staff and patients alike started to run in various directions.

"The hippos are loose," someone shouted. "In the hospital! Everyone must return to their rooms and shut and lock your doors."

She'd heard rumors of a marsh on campus filled with, hippos. She imagined they were usually confined to their ecosystem, but somehow, they were being shepherded into WANC. More specifically into the hospital wing. This couldn't be an accident.

"Hurry," the red-haired nurse urged, standing up from his chair.

Lyla and Gabby did as instructed, each fleeing in opposite directions, toward their own rooms. Lyla was glad the floor was smooth so her IV pole easily slid with her, not catching on anything in the panic.

The noise had barely faded when Lyla made it to her room and shut the door behind her. Not surprisingly, it sounded like a herd of hippos were stomping down the hall. The linoleum shook under her feet while the water in the glass on the table bounced around and the pebble next to it fell to the floor. Lyla opened her door a crack as a hippo bounded past. She shut the door and relocked it, pressing her back to it as her mind ran in various directions.

This was too convenient. And what timing. Right before she'd tried to get word to FUC and ASS about the strange worm she'd seen, disaster struck.

Suddenly, it occurred to her that she and Gabby should have stayed together. What if this was a distraction for the intruder—or the Dr. Grimm Gabby mentioned— to snatch her friend? Her heart pounded in her chest. They should have come to Lyla's room together. She shouldn't have risked leaving Gabby alone, especially after promising she'd keep her safe.

Well, that was a promise she intended to keep, so she'd have to do something about it now.

But how would she get down the hallway without being spotted by a hippo? The things were ginormous and danger-ous. They could gulp her down in two bites. Maybe one, if it was a bigger hippo. Goodbye, Lyla.

Maybe there was a way she could make it to Gabby's room without becoming a snack. She looked to her trusty IV bag. "I think it's time we parted ways for a little bit." She sighed. She was only permitted to shift under doctor super-vision at the moment, and she hadn't tried shifting more than once in any one day.

But if the loud ruckus outside her door was any indica-tion of how well wrangling the hippos was going, she guessed things were pretty dire. Gabby needed her.

Lyla smiled at her IV bag. "Well, here goes nothing." She disconnected the line. Lyla peeled off her clothes and threw them onto the hospital bed. She tiptoed to the door, afraid the hippos outside would sense her. She opened the door a few inches and stepped back.

It'd been a while since she shifted without supervision.

Was her body replenished enough to be able to make the transition for the second time in one day? She'd find out.

She called forward the familiar sensation. First a tingling. Then an ache followed by goosebumps across her skin that slowly sprouted feathers. Like tiny saplings springing forth from the ground after planting a garden, her plumage sprang up from her skin. Her body began to shrink simultaneously. The ache in her bones grew as they became less dense. A bird couldn't fly with human bones. Everything in her body had to change. Even her heartbeat sped up.

Exhaustion set it. It was the slowest shift of her life, but she did it. Lyla perched on the table next to her hospital bed. Now was the real test. Could she fly? Her wings flapped about eighty times per second. That'd put a strain on her new glucose reserves for sure. But Gabby was worth it. If Lyla made it there, that was. And that wasn't even thinking about the chances of her becoming hippo lunch.

Lyla willed her tiny wings to flap. At first, it wasn't enough to get her off the table. She sputtered around like a baby bird learning to take flight. A hop here, a hover there. As she kept at it, her wings settled into their usual rhythm. After liftoff, she tucked her little bird legs under her. If she could take it slow, she would've hovered a bit before heading out of her room, but there was no time. Gabby could be in danger. At the very least, she was alone and frightened.

She sped toward the open door, flying out into the hall. She narrowly escaped the jaws of a hippo eating dirty sheets and hospital gowns in the hamper of a nearby cart. It chomped away, swallowing the fabric whole, letting out a large burp after sucking down the tie of a bathrobe like a spaghetti noodle. The scene was something from a B horror film.

She sped past that one, seeing the chaos behind. Equipment lay knocked over on the floor. A mess of knotted cords with gauze and syringes sprinkled on top, like a hospital supply sundae, sat in the corner by the nurses' station. A nurse stood on the counter, swatting at a smaller hippo with a broom. The creature seemed to think it was a game, dodging the blows before getting bored and grabbing the broom with its massive jaws. The handle snapped in half as it chomped down. The nurse gave a high-pitched squeak before running away to take refuge in a nearby vacant room as the hippo continued to crunch the broom like it was a giant pretzel rod.

Lyla's wings began to ache from the strain on her muscles to pump as fast as they needed to in order to float her down the hall. She stayed near the ceiling, not wanting another close call with the giant maws of a hippo. She realized belatedly that she wasn't sure how she'd open the door to Gabby's room, but she'd cross that bridge when she got there. Hopefully, it wasn't locked—the door, not the proverbial bridge.

The cart filled with lunch was parked next to Gabby's room. How unfortunate. She wasn't sure what hippos ate in the wild, but the ones from FUCN'A seemed to enjoy grilled cheese sandwiches and pudding. If Lyla's plan had been to turn back into a human to open the door, she certainly couldn't safely do that with the hippo camped out, snacking on the patients' lunches. What would lure a hippo away? Even more importantly, how could she do that as a hummingbird?

Lyla looked to the trays. Maybe if she disguised herself as a tasty snack, the beast would follow her. If hippos lived in the marsh, maybe they liked vegetation. It was worth a shot anyway. She spied a salad on the lower shelf of the cart. She zipped down on tiny wings, careful to avoid the snapping mouth of the hippo. She burrowed in the lettuce, hoping some of the leaves would stick to her. She grabbed a large piece in her beak. Flying with it proved difficult. The salad debris made her less aerodynamic, and her dropping energy levels wouldn't manage the extra weight for long. She would have to make it work. She was determined to make it work.

She fluttered toward the nostril of the large hippo as it was about to taste the tomato soup. It lapped up a mouthful before grimacing. Apparently, that wasn't to the liking of the creature. Hopefully the lettuce in her beak would be.

She waved the leaf in front of the beast's nose. Its nostrils dilated as it sniffed after her. The inhalation nearly sucked Lyla into the face of the hippo. She quickly flapped away. The ground shook as it followed, its large paws stomping on overthrown trays of food and garbage, squishing the refuse between its toes.

Jaws snapped at Lyla as she lured the hippo down the hall. It moved faster than she intended. Or maybe that was because she was slowing down. She was no longer able to zip around like normal. Her energy reserves were burning up quickly. If she had a meter that showed how full her gas tank was, the needle would be hovering awfully close to E.

She dropped the lettuce from her beak as she spotted a metal rack of shelves up ahead against the wall. She flew toward it, soaring through the lowest level. After hiding behind a box of bandages and gauze, Lyla peeked around the corner to see where the hippo ended up. Its jaws snapped down on the opposite end of the broom the smaller hippo was munching on. The pair played tug-o-war with the pole.

Lyla took this as her cue to zoom as fast as her tired little wings could carry her to Gabby's room. Midair, she transformed back into her naked human form. She landed on her feet with a thud. She didn't judge the landing right. Her ankle made a nauseating popping sound, nearly giving out on her. She ignored the pain and twisted the door handle. With a click, the door swung open. Lyla rushed in, slamming the door behind her before she took in the state of the room.

She gasped at what she saw.

The overturned hospital bed lay on top of the scatter of word puzzle books on the floor. The fluorescent reading light over the bed flickered, the plastic cover now a spiderweb of cracks as if someone—or something—had crashed into it. This couldn't have been the work of a hippo. They couldn't open and close doors.

"Gabby?" She waited for a response, crossing her arms across her bare chest to keep the cold out. Goosebumps—or more accurately hummingbird bumps—erupted across her flesh with the cool air the air conditioner was pumping out. As she took another step, something hard dug into her foot. "Ouch!" She hopped over it. A small black object the size of a rock sat on the floor. She crouched down and picked it up. It was a hard plastic figurine. Of a crow.

Lyla turned around, searching for the tray table that slid across the bed. She figured since the crow had appeared after Gabby's visit with her family, it must have been a gift from them, and Lyla didn't want it getting broken. That was when she noticed the glass in the window was gone. The jagged remains of glass jutted out of the pane like the long canine teeth of the hippos in the hallway. Except, unlike the hippos, these glass fangs were pointed at the ends.

Lyla glanced at the floor, expecting to see glass strewn across it. Aside from the mess of the books, bed sheets, and bed, the floor was clean. The cold linoleum bit into Lyla's soles, sending a shiver up her bare back. She crept closer to the window.

"Gabby?" she tried again, though her voice nearly failed her. It caught in her throat, nearly drying up like her depleted stamina.

A warm breeze greeted her from the broken window. It was oddly pleasant and unexpected in the chaos of the hospital wing. Lyla's heart hammered rapidly in her chest as if she were still in hummingbird form. "Gabby?" The whisper of air barely crossed her lips.

She looked out the window, hoping to find Gabby in the courtyard. Aside from the missing tray table and picnic tables farther down, the courtyard was empty. It appeared to Lyla that someone had thrown the small table out the window to break the glass. Could it have been Gabby? Did she not trust that her room would be safe from the hippos and tried to get out?

Lyla wanted to hope so, because the alternative was so much worse.

As Lyla's knees gave out, she was struck with a terrible revelation. Gabby was gone.

9

———

Gabby's eyes fluttered open to darkness. A familiar musty smell wafted up her nostrils. This couldn't be possible. The subterranean lab where she was kept was raided and shut down by FUC and ASS. Or so she thought.

Bright lights came to life above her. They bathed the small room in a white glow, illuminating a hospital bed, small metal table, and toilet and sink in the corner. This was another cell. Fear bubbled up inside of her, threatening to spill the contents of her stomach onto the floor. Anxiety buzzed in her chest, squeezing her heart. Her breaths came in shallow gasps, and she sat up, moving to the edge of the bed to try to wrangle her panic. Focusing on taking deep breaths, Gabby exhaled slowly through her mouth, letting her diaphragm push the air out. Nice and slow. One more breath filled her, slowing her heart back down to a more normal rhythm. She let it out gently, deflating her belly. Her jumbled thoughts untangled themselves, floating by at a more leisurely pace. She wiped her sweaty palms on the hospital gown, taking the time to notice the soft fabric. The panic ebbed to high anxiety, but at least she could function again.

She scratched at the back of her neck, trying to ascertain how this could be possible. Gabby racked her brain for her last memory. It was fuzzy and kept swimming just out of focus. She tried to piece it together. Lyla was in her room, and they'd gone to the nurses' station together. Lyla was going to help her tell Agent Stone about Dr. Grimm! Then a loud commotion broke out in the hallway, and they'd each run for their rooms. Gabby had made it to hers, but she wasn't alone. A tiny creature hobbled toward her. It looked like a mole with long whiskers, except its snout was too long. And it didn't have shovel-like paws on its forelegs for digging. This was no mole.

That was when she noticed its tail, long, thick, and hairless. It immediately reminded her of the worm Lyla had mentioned. *Is this what Lyla saw when she went to the library?*

Before she could decide how to react to the creature, a giant hippo came into view in the hallway. Gabby had no choice but to shut the door, keeping the tiny rat-like critter in with her. The thing was so small, so what harm could it do?

But then it grew in size. Its grey fur receded as its limbs lengthened. The rat-like tail shrank until it vanished. Tan skin stretched across the frame of a young man. His face wrinkled in concern as if fighting some internal battle.

Gabby took a step back, bumping into her hospital bed. She didn't know who this stranger was, but she didn't trust him. Especially if it was the same creature Lyla spotted earlier creeping around the building.

"I'm sorry for this." The young man inspected her with his green eyes.

"For what?" she asked, but that was when the memory cut out. Something happened between her room and this cell. And that man had something to do with it. She glanced around her new surroundings. She had to figure a way out. But where was she?

"Welcome back! It's so good to see you again," a thin, familiar voice spat out from the tiny speaker on the wall. She pictured the too-white teeth in the mouth that broadcast that voice through the intercom system. "Sorry I had to send my shrew after you. He's a little rough around the edges for my taste, but he's so good at finding things—and subverting FUCN'A security measures."

Gabby's core burned at the amusement she heard in Dr. Grimm's voice. He spoke as if catching up with an old friend. She wanted to rip the speaker off the wall.

"Why!" Gabby shouted in frustration, not knowing if the speaker was two-way or not.

"You'll find I perfected our serum," Dr. Grimm explained.

"What you… talking about?" She let her anger hone her focus, helping her tie into the singing part of her brain. "Let me go!" Her shrill voice hit the walls around her, rattling the small window in the door of her cell. The words came out like a singer belting out a song on Broadway. She couldn't savor the sentence. Whatever he'd perfected, it was bad news for her. Gabby had to find a way out before he tried his new serum on her.

"Gabrielle, you were always my favorite."

She hated the sound of the smile on his lips. Hated the way his voice sounded thin, like his vocal cords were stretched too tight, ready to snap. What Gabby hated most of all was the way this prick thought he could do whatever he wanted to her, without her permission.

Not again.

She picked up the small, metal table, throwing it at the door with a scream. She'd played the docile captive last time, and it got her nowhere. She wouldn't make that mistake twice.

The table hit the concrete floor with a clang. She trudged to the door, picking the table up again. She dragged it across the floor behind her, ready to throw it again.

"I wouldn't do that if I were you," the disembodied voice of Dr. Grimm cautioned over the speaker.

"Why. The. Fuck. Not." She didn't want to give Dr. Grimm the satisfaction of watching her struggle to talk. Gabby swallowed between words and focused with all her might. She used all the tools Lynn had given her over the past year.

"Because your anger will speed up the mutation. It could be painful."

"What… the fuck… you…" Searing pain cut through the skin of her upper back. It was as if someone had taken a whip, striking her. The flesh across her shoulders stung. The table fell from her hands. It hit the ground with a thick clatter missing her feet by a few centimeters. She nearly fell on top of it when the burning sensation began. It was too late. He'd already dosed her with his toxic cocktail while she was unconscious. "What…did you…do to me?!" she roared.

"Gabrielle, my angel, calm down. There's no need for violence." His voice made her want to do anything but.

Focusing proved difficult with the unbearable pain spreading across her upper back. It felt like she was being ripped from the inside out. This must be how childbirth felt to mothers. How the hell did anyone do that voluntarily? Blades cutting through her skin would have hurt less.

She grabbed the table and threw it again, smashing it into the door. This time, a spiderweb of cracks spread across the glass in long, thin fingers. She cocked her head sideways. Did she throw the table harder that time? Or was it her imagination?

A scream blasted out of her mouth as another burst of pain dropped her to her knees. A warm trickle of blood, hot and sticky, slid down her back. She tried to reach for the table, but her shoulder blades hurt too bad. There was too much tension across her skin. She reached back to investigate. Short, round protrusion poked out of the tears in her skin. No wonder it felt like her back would rip open if she stretched for the table. Something had broken through her skin and was growing.

She glanced around, looking for the camera. There had to be one. It seemed that aside from being able to hear her, Dr. Grimm could see the transformation as well. At the very least, she'd rob him of that satisfaction.

Up in the corner above the intercom, she spotted a small, round camera lens. Fuck her back. She'd heal.

Gabby picked up the table and launched it where the corner of the wall met the ceiling of her cell. It smashed into the camera, and the device burst into a handful of pieces. There was no denying it now. She was stronger. There was no way she'd have been able to throw a metal table that high prior to whatever Dr. Grimm did to her.

The protrusions in her back lengthened. The flesh of her back tingled as it spread across the new bones forming. Soon long spires jutted out of her shoulder blades. The sensation was similar to when her arms turned into wings when she shifted into her crow. The materials of her body rearranged themselves, morphing into something similar. In this case, creating something new.

She thought back to what Dr. Grimm had said moments ago. *Gabrielle, my angel...* Did he give her wings in human form? Like an angel? Her thoughts went to a woman she'd heard of named Nevaeh. She was a legend around the rehab wing. A woman who'd been considered an angel or a harpy. She couldn't exactly remember which was true and the topic seemed up for debate.

She didn't have time to think about Nevaeh, though. The

scorching pain finally let up and the skin of her back quickly healed, stitching itself back together, sealing the gash the new bones piercing her back had left. New muscle and flesh knit together, forming a covering to the once bare bones. The familiar tingling of feathers erupting from the new skin spread across the large wings.

She'd end the good doctor herself if given the chance.

She grabbed her trusty table again. Without the terrible pain, picking it up wasn't so bad. Instead of throwing it, she decided to use it like a baseball bat, swinging it over and over again at the tiny glass until it shattered into a million pieces. The space she created was too small for human Gabby to fit out of, but it was the right size for a crow to fly through. If she could shift. Who knew what other changes the doctor's new formula had made? She hoped the new wings were the extent of it.

She shut her eyes, focusing on the bird inside of her. Her bones shrank and hollowed out, turning into light bird bones. The awkward and heavy wings compressed, sizing down as the rest of her body did. But instead of her arms turning into wings—as was usual for her shift—to her dismay, they merely shrank. Gabby thought they'd disappear, but she wasn't so lucky. *At least I don't have two sets of wings— that would be weird. And awkward.*

But right now, that was the least of her worries. She had to get the fuck out of Dodge before the doctor did something else to her.

Aside from the tiny human arms on her bird body, Gabby found herself in crow form. She tucked her arms under her wings, doing her best to sink them into her soft, black feathers. How she was going to fly was beyond her. She thought back to her childhood. Since Dad was also a crow, he'd taught her to fly. He'd explained that wings worked differently than arms. The bones linked together, bending and flexing in a way that arms couldn't.

She remembered those first shifts. They were uncomfortable, and she'd been so clumsy. It was the equivalent of learning to ride a bike. But she didn't give up. Her dad helped her to learn how to use her wings, how to flap them when gaining altitude, and how to hold them out to glide.

It was now or never. Gabby's bird legs took a few tiny steps as she flapped first her arms by mistake then her wings. Before, when she shifted, her human arms moved and turned into her crow wings. Now her arms had merely shrunk, and a new set of limbs remained as her wings. It was like trying to pat your head and rub your tummy at the same time. She brought all her focus to her two sets of upper limbs. Tuck the arms, flap the wings.

Soon she had enough momentum for takeoff. Her altitude was too low to float through the window, so she did a lap of the room first. She noticed the window wouldn't allow her wingspan through. She'd have to dive.

Gabby did an extra lap to make sure she had enough speed—and practice—before attempting the maneuver. *This could go very wrong.* She could splat on the side of the door or knock herself out of the air. Then she'd be gift-wrapping herself for Dr. Asshole.

Gabby eyed up the opening and lined herself up just above it. She flapped toward it. At the last second, she tucked her wings back into a dive. Like jumping through a hoop, she javelined herself through the window. Once sure she was on the other side, she opened her wings to soar before she crashed into the ground. The strange new wings pushed her up into the air like a kite.

"Gabby!" Dr. Grimm called from the other end of the hall.

It took all her focus to not fly after him to scratch his eyes out. Anger would lead to mistakes. That would cause her to get caught. Again.

She banked right and flapped away from the yelling doctor. Whether the rooms lining the hall were vacant or filled, she didn't know. Didn't have time to stop. She'd tell FUC and ASS about this place later. If she was able to fully escape. *One thing at a time*, she reminded herself.

Her side feathers didn't do much to cover the human arms. She fought back a shiver from the cool air blowing across her naked limbs. The violent motion of that could rip her out of the air. Instead, she tried to nestle her arms deeper into the feathers. A feat that proved beyond her talent or practice. She lost altitude. In a panic, she started flapping her arms by mistake, her wings helplessly moving in a way that didn't keep her afloat. She could not guide her body through the air and lost control. Gabby hit the door at the end of the corridor with a thud. One side of her body ached from the blow.

She shook it off, ruffling up her feathers before changing back. Gabby looked human aside from the large wings poking out of her back. She needed regular-sized hands and body to open the door but had every intention of shifting again to fly away from this hell hole. After flinging it open, knocking her right wing on the doorframe as she ran through before slamming the door shut behind her. Without missing a beat, Gabby ran up the stairway. It looped around like the stairs of a lighthouse. Running in a spiral made her dizzy. Blackness entered her field of vision, but she refused to succumb to the nausea. Her bare feet pounded on the cold metal. Up and up she climbed. Her lungs burned, her ribs ached, and she felt a new stitch in her side. If she could power through wings growing out of her back, she'd survive this.

The stairs popped her up into a narrow chamber with a

lone door at the far end. She kept her legs pumping away, closing the distance. She pulled the next door open, nearly collapsing with joy as the warm rays of the sun kissed her skin. Without taking too much time to survey the surroundings, Gabby shifted back into crow form. Once the transformation was complete, she willed her arms to tuck and the new wings to flap after a few mishaps of moving the wrong set, keeping a steady pace with her bird feet before taking flight.

She saw the aggravation on Dr. Grimm's face as he burst out the door seconds behind her. Still ignoring the urge to claw—or peck—out his beady little eyes, Gabby soared higher. She enjoyed the warm sun soaking into her sable feathers. Freedom tasted sweeter than revenge.

10

An army of custodians mopped, vacuumed, swept, and waxed the hospital floors after the hippos were lured away and put back in their marsh. The mess they left behind would take most of the night to clean. Food, supplies, and clothing torn and trampled sat in messy piles nearly everywhere. It looked like a horde of giant toddlers had been left unsupervised for hours and trashed the place.

Lyla sipped the hot chocolate—not for pleasure, but out of necessity to replenish her sugar reserves—as Agent Stone and Sparks bombarded her with questions.

A trickle of sweat slid down the side of her face, and she pushed the sleeves of her sweater up to her elbows. Since bodies burned more energy trying to stay warm, Dr. Brown had instructed the staff to turn the air conditioning to her room off. She didn't want to risk Lyla being too cold while she recuperated. A pile of sugary foods and drinks sat on the table next to her bed, waiting to be consumed. And boy was she hungry.

"That's when you noticed Gabby was gone?" Agent

Sparks dabbed at the sweat on her own forehead before brushing a red curl out of her face. Her medium brown skin seemed kissed with gold as the setting sun shimmered across her face.

Lyla nodded. Various agents had her retelling her tale all afternoon. When she mentioned the worm, they made her wait for Agents Stone and Sparks. When they finally arrived, they wanted to hear everything from the beginning. Lyla started with her trip to the library, the worm sighting, and then the hungry, hungry hippo exhibit in the hallway of the hospital. Her tale ended with finding Gabby missing and the state of her room.

"Back to the worm." Agent Stone's brown eyes narrowed. "Did you see the front of it?"

"No…" Lyla cocked her head sideways. She thought back to what Gabby had pointed out. *Worms don't flop.* "Maybe it wasn't a worm after all. Could it be something's giant mutant tail? Like a rat?"

Agent Stone and Agent Sparks exchanged a knowing glance, something unspoken passing between them. "We had Agent Kipp scan the security cameras. I cannot reveal what he found, but he did identify the species of intruder we were looking for earlier. We can have him recheck for anything else out of the ordinary in case we missed something during the ordeal." Agent Stone slid the tiny notebook into his breast pocket.

"You mean the hippos charging through the halls?" Lyla snickered.

Agent Sparks rifled through her purse before setting a card on the table next to the smorgasbord of sugar. "Here, so you can have our cell numbers. We want you to reach out to us if you think of anything else."

Without another word, they left Lyla to her food. Lyla

polished off the hot chocolate. She eyed up the rest of the treats, but it seemed weird to be eating food she associated with celebration when her friend was missing. Her stomach growled in protest. *All right.* She supposed she could eat some of the dew melon. Maybe drink more of the apple juice. She needed to replenish her energy. Feeling bad about herself or blaming herself for Gabby's disappearance would get her nowhere. It definitely wouldn't get Gabby back.

A thought occurred to her. If she could gain her strength back, she could fly out to try to track down Gabby. The more eyes looking for her, the better. Though there were a few ASS agents on the job, it couldn't hurt to have an extra bird out there.

But how much of a risk would it be to shift again?

She glanced to her IV bag, which had been plugged back into her hand, and sighed. It didn't feel like she was starting over, but it felt like she erased most of her progress.

No. That wasn't true. She didn't feel overly exhausted. When she'd first arrived at WANC, the numb fingers of fatigue gripped her brain, threatening to pull her back into sleep. She passed out so easily from exhaustion in the beginning. After her first interrogation by the agents, she slept a whole day. But now…

Lyla looked from the pile of food to the window. The sun was beginning its descent, sending pink and purple rays out from the pastel horizon. She'd need all night to get her strength back up.

All she could do was hope that Gabby was okay.

Gabby struggled to sleep with the creaking branches around her. She tried to brush it off as the wind, but she shuddered to think what would happen if Dr. Grimm found her again. She nestled further down into the vacant nest she'd found, glad its occupants didn't need it tonight. Her human arms were crossed tightly across her chest, trying to keep in the warmth. Though the summer day was hot, the night air didn't hold much heat. The oak tree where she tried to sleep didn't offer much protection from the wind. She'd never tried to sleep as a crow before. That probably wasn't helping. She feared she'd turn back into a human in her sleep and fall out of the tree.

The bough shuddered under the nest as a gust of wind caught it. How did real birds do it? It was terrifying. Her mind filled with images of her falling asleep just before the breeze knocked her out of the tree. The anxious thought ended with Dr. Grimm waiting at the bottom for her, ready to scoop her up into a tiny birdcage. A shiver trickled down her spine just thinking of it.

In her mind, Gabby plotted her course back to WANC. As a bird, she could tell exactly where she was by using the Earth's magnetic field as a compass. Though it wasn't as easy as using a GPS or map, she knew what direction she needed to start heading in tomorrow, but not necessarily how far she had to go. She wanted to put as much distance as possible between her and Dr. Grimm. With any luck, she'd lose him before getting back to FUCN'A. Then the agents could deal with him.

She watched the silver moonlight trickle through the long oak leaves, leaving dark shadows around her. Gabby liked the dark. With her black feathers, she could easily hide, blending into the darkness. She could use the night as a blanket. But during the day, it would be more challenging. Though there were many crows and ravens in this area, she had a feeling she was the only one sporting human arms.

Gabby tried to keep her eyes on the moon, watching it slip farther toward the west. Soon her eyes grew heavy, and even the wind couldn't keep her awake. She needed her rest if she were to face Dr. Grimm again tomorrow. If he found her once, he'd be able to do it again.

11

———————

The golden rays of dawn gently brushed across Gabby's eyelids. She opened her eyes to a pink sunrise. The color was a perfect match to Lyla's hair. Gabby had a sinking feeling in her gut that she'd never see her friend again. Suddenly, she regretted that she hadn't asked Lyla to go to the party. The thought became needles in her brain. She shook the feeling away as her tummy growled. There wasn't time to forage for food. She needed to get back. And fast.

She stretched out all four of her upper limbs. It was slightly easier to control them but still awkward at times. Occasionally her brain signaled the wrong set to move. She nearly fell from the air a few times last night before spotting the vacant nest in the oak tree. With a shake, she ruffled all her feathers, ready to face whatever horrors the new day might bring. Hopefully none, but it didn't hurt to be prepared. Gabby found it best to lean toward being realistic instead of optimistic.

Her sharp eyes scanned the ground for any creature that didn't seem to belong. Robins and chickadees hopped around, searching for worms. The morning welcomed her like an old friend. Birds chirped and called all around. Before taking flight, she scanned the skies. A hawk flew in lazy circles above the yellowing grass of the nearby field. Her stomach leaped into her chest. Sandy, her previous captor from last year, shifted into a red-tailed hawk. But this one appeared to be of the wild variety. When Sandy shifted, she was a human-sized bird. This creature could easily perch on the outstretched arm of a person. And while hawks sometimes did go after smaller birds as prey, Gabby was a crow. They were seldom bothered by birds of prey.

Nothing seemed out of the ordinary. And if there was anything she'd taken away from camping as a kid, it was that if the birds were chirping, there were probably no predators —or pesky humans—lurking about. The songbirds urged her out of the nest with their cheerful melodies. She needed an early start to the day to get back to WANC and ask for help. If she could make it that far. Gabby wasn't used to solely navigating as a bird. True, she took small trips around her neighborhood, pre-kidnapping, that was. To her, it was like taking a walk around the block. But she never flew distances this great. And she was a year out of practice. But what choice did she have?

She spread her arms and nearly hopped out of the nest to her death. So much for having control of her new limbs. Then a crazy thought occurred to her. What if she shifted back and flew while in human—or was it now angel— form? Could she travel faster that way? Maybe. But it wouldn't be safe. Who knew what could happen if the humans caught sight of a naked woman, soaring through the skies on black wings. They'd think the end of days had come. She could possibly start a panic. No. It was easier to be a crow even it if took her longer to get back. Plus, she didn't want to think about the trouble she'd be in trying to explain to both FUC and ASS why she thought it would be a great idea to fly around looking like an angel who forgot her heavenly robes. She'd be in big, big trouble for sure.

Not to mention, that semi-shifted form would make it easier for Dr. Asshole to find her.

Part of her wanted to be found, though. She wanted to make him pay. He needed to never hurt anyone again. She would break him like he'd almost broken her. She shook her head, swallowing up the wickedness that wanted to bubble up inside her. Gabby couldn't cross that line. She wasn't a bad guy like those who hurt her and the others.

After quite a bit of focus, Gabby spread her wings and took to the skies.

Her shoulders ached from flying. The hot sun rained down heat from its zenith, baking her black feathers. Gabby needed a break. If her bird body could sweat, she would.

She spread her wings, feeling the breeze trickle through the edge of her feathers as she floated down back to the Earth. The heat from the ground below rushed up at her as she neared the edge of a field bordering a park. Children ran, chasing each other across the playground. Gabby would have to stay away from them or risk someone seeing her arms.

A seagull gulped down water from a puddle in the parking lot. She walked over, eyeing the water. She could see the bottom, and it didn't smell bad. It had rained the other day, so hopefully it was fresh enough for her to drink. She leaned over it, letting her black beak scoop up some hydration. The seagull gave her a sidelong glance, squawking at her human arms. She gave it her middle finger. The bird blinked before taking off. Maybe the arms were useful. She cawed out a chuckle before lapping again at the water.

She glanced up between sips. The humans took no notice

of her, but the birds stood clear. A set of robins gave a shrill cry in her direction before taking off. It was a call to warn other birds of possible danger. Was she what they were all afraid of? Or was something else amiss?

The children continued to play in the distance. It looked like a new game. Instead of tag, they tried to get around the park without touching the ground. Some parents watched their kids, chuckling to themselves, while others played on their cellphones. No one took notice of the crow with arms drinking from a puddle.

Maybe she didn't smell like a bird, and that had the fowl keeping their distance. Though most birds didn't have a good sense of smell. She leaned in to take another swig of the warm water but noticed a shadow in the reflection. Something tall stood behind her.

She ran as fast as her bird legs would carry her under the bumper of a nearby car as a pair of arms swooped toward her. The hands splashed in the puddle. The hem of the man's khaki pants was just visible beneath the bumper of the vehicle where Gabby hid as he crooned, "I'm not going to hurt you."

The hell you aren't. She'd heard that voice before. In her hospital room. And after her last run-in with the shrew, Dr. Grimm gave her wings. Who knew what other concoctions the lunatic wanted to try out on her next? No thank you.

"Ow. *Ow!*" the young man suddenly yelled. Gabby peeked her head out from under the vehicle to see a bright pink hummingbird stabbing the man over and over with its long, needle-like beak.

Lyla! It must be!

The man flapped his arms, but the bird was too fast. She pursued him, not stopping until he was well out of the park. Then the little bird zoomed back to Gabby, landing on the ground beside the parked car.

Gabby observed the tiny bird's chest heaving with exhaustion, but she wasn't ready to rest. With a tiny buzz, Lyla ushered Gabby away from the parking lot and the screaming children in the park to the tiny slip of woods beyond. She looked from Gabby to the greenery beyond. Gabby understood her meaning. With any luck, they could find a place to hide and work out a plan. The two took to the air, landing in the brush of the small forest.

Before Gabby could caw a thank-you, the hummingbird transformed. It grew in size, losing all its brilliant feathers, with the exception of the ones around its head. Soon Lyla was standing before her, naked, sweat glistening on her olive-toned skin. She leaned an arm on a nearby tree, struggling to catch her breath. Gabby thought back to the IV bag that always accompanied Lyla. Hummingbirds were known to need a lot of energy to move as fast as they did, and if Lyla's captivity was anything like Gabby's, she was barely fed. That would mean Lyla risked physical burnout to find her. She could have easily run out of energy and gotten stranded somewhere.

Gabby shifted and threw herself toward Lyla in one swift motion. She needed her to know how thankful she was for the rescue and how relieved she was to see her again.

After knocking the tops of her wings on a low branch, she threw her arms around Lyla, sobbing into her sweet-smelling hair. Lyla's warm and safe body welcomed her. It was so good to be with her friend again, but it didn't solve everything. Most specifically, *How soon before he finds me again?*

12

———

"How?" Gabby sobbed into Lyla's neck.

Lyla gently stroked Gabby's unkempt hair, willing her heart rate to slow. She wiped the sweat off her forehead with the back of her hand.

"I talked with the shifter birds I came across." Many had given a warning of a crow who didn't seem a crow. Lyla figured it would have to be Gabby, though she was caught off guard when she saw her in bird form with little human arms. She gulped, trying to find the courage to state the obvious. "Word spreads quickly when..." Her voice trailed off. She looked to the black wings sprouting out of Gabby's back. The woman had been through Hell more than once, yet here she stood before her, a smile on her face as if none of it mattered.

"Crow with arms," Gabby finished as a dark look clouded her blue eyes.

"Yeah." Lyla stroked the hair out of Gabby's eyes. She bit her lip, glancing in the direction of the park. They were hidden where they were, but that creep could easily circle back to find them. Who was that jerk anyway?

As if reading her mind, Gabby said, "Shrew. Found me."

"Shrew?" Lyla understood the second part, but what the hell was a shrew?

"Tail. Not worm."

Then it all made sense. What Lyla had seen outside the library, which the agents hinted was a creature—apparently a shrew—had a worm-like tail. She felt her brow wrinkle up in confusion. "But how did he find you?"

Gabby shrugged. "Dr. Grimm said…" Her nose crinkled as she focused. Lyla let her have as much time as she needed, admiring how cute her face looked when she focused. "Shrew good at finding… things." She huffed out a breath.

Lyla squeezed Gabby's arms with a smile. "That was a long sentence." This time, instead of pointing out her inability to focus, Gabby leaned in, pressing her lips to Lyla's. The touch of Gabby's lips sent a buzzing excitement through Lyla's body. She felt she could fly for a thousand miles if needed. She'd stab all the shrews in the world with her beak if it meant Gabby would kiss her again.

She leaned into the kiss, wrapping her arms around Gabby, careful not to bump the new wings. The touch of Gabby's smooth skin built a fire beneath hers, flames licking under the surface, threatening to consume her. She parted her lips, letting Gabby in to taste her. Their tongues twirled in a rhythmic dance, hungry for more. Her clit tingled, aching for Gabby to taste it next. Then for her to taste Gabby next. Lyla wanted nothing more than for this moment to last forever, for their bodies to be entwined with the heat of passion.

But she pulled away.

"I want this. I want you," she managed to squeak out between huffing breaths. "But it's not safe here. We need to get back."

Gabby nodded, though the heat of the moment burned in her eyes. Lyla had to peel herself away from that look. It took all the strength within her to not kneel in the dirt and taste the warmth between Gabby's legs, worshiping her the way she deserved. Instead, Lyla leaned forward, pressing a kiss to Gabby's forehead. A gentle promise that her feelings were more than lust and longing.

"It's a long way back to WANC, but I'll let you know if I need any breaks." She forced a smile. Lyla had no idea if she could make it ten feet. She looked to Gabby. She had to keep her safe. She mustered up all the positive feelings she had about Gabby and used them to propel herself back into hummingbird form. Hopefully, they'd pass something sugary to eat.

From a nearby branch, Lyla watched Gabby transform. She struggled with the arms and wings. It seemed like she kept moving the wrong set. Lyla chirped out encouragement as Gabby got ready to take off. After a few irritated caws, Gabby took to the air. Lyla fluttered her wings, catching up before taking the lead. She crossed her toes, hoping they'd be able to make it back to the shifter hospital before anything bad happened. Like Lyla falling out of the sky from exhaustion.

They managed to cover a great distance before Lyla needed to stop. From the air, she spotted rows of short trees. Her wings stalled, dropping her altitude quickly. Gabby cawed from behind, noticing Lyla's plight. Her tank was beyond empty. With any luck, an orchard of some sort was below them. She chirped back, signaling she wanted to land. After doing a fly-by, she picked a section of trees at the center that had the least likelihood of them being spotted by any unwanted guests. It would be a pain in the ass to explain why the two women were naked. It would be even more annoying to tell the agents back at FUCN'A that they needed to fill out more paperwork to cover up the incident. It would be even worse if a regular human saw them transform.

Scratch that. It would be worse if Dr. Grimm or the shrew found them. Then they'd be back at square one. Lyla had no energy to deal with any of that.

After changing back into human form, Lyla grabbed an apple from a nearby tree. She gripped the firm red and orange fruit in her hand. She could almost feel the sugar inside. She salivated with what little saliva she had left at the thought of her teeth piercing the skin of the apple.

The hot sun winking through the gnarled leafy boughs of the tree warmed up her flesh, almost too much. Her skin felt on fire from the heat of exhaustion and the summer sun. She sat in the shade of the tree, careful to not sit on any twigs. That was the last thing she needed—a stick to the hoo-haw.

Gabby pressed the back of her hand onto Lyla's clammy forehead, kneeling next to her. Her dark brows winkled in concern, adding a gentle maternal beauty to her face. "Y-you okay?" She didn't have to make a complete sentence for Lyla to know Gabby had asked how depleted were her energy reserves. Worry clouded her blue eyes as they passed over Lyla's sweaty frame. She knew Lyla wasn't doing well.

Lyla bit into the juicy apple, rejoicing in the sugar fix. Its tart flavor tingled on her tongue. She swallowed, her mouth almost too dry to do so. "It's only a few more miles."

"Travel as humans?" Gabby raised an eyebrow before fighting with her wings. Instead of tucking her wings in to sit next to Lyla, she crossed her arms. Her feathers caught in the low, gnarled branches. With a huff, she shook them loose, showering leaves on both of them.

"Where would we find clothes? Neither one of us has a mobile phone to order NAKED. And how would we hide those?" Lyla pointed to the large wings Gabby struggled to sit with.

A pink blush spread across her pale cheeks. Gabby probably forgot she couldn't pass for human anymore. Lyla kicked herself for not instead saying that the pink feathers on her own head could be problematic. She leaned her head on Gabby's shoulder. "I'm sorry."

Gabby lifted Lyla's chin with her finger. "Don't be... You... didn't... do... this." She spat out each word after a long pause, but she managed to string together a longer sentence than usual.

"Do you want to go to the party with me? Huggie's party? If we ever get out of here?" The words tumbled out of Lyla's mouth. A nervousness bubbled in her stomach. Maybe it was hunger. She was too tired to tell.

"I would. Love to." Gabby's pink lips stretched back into a smile, lighting up her dirty face. "Now eat," she chided, pointing to the unfinished apple in Lyla's hand.

Lyla beamed back at her. Even though they were on the run from a shrew henchman and an evil doctor and currently sitting naked beneath an apple tree, she couldn't have been happier. She took another bite. "I'll probably need five of these before we can leave." She chuckled, savoring the bitter-sweetness of the under-ripe apple.

Gabby laughed, the tips of her wings shaking with each breath. The golden sun shimmered in each of the sable feathers. Even her new wings were beautiful. Lyla wanted to curl up in Gabby's lap and bask in the heat of the summer day. But she had to get her energy up. Again. She prayed for the day when activity didn't take everything out of her.

The lactic acid buildup in her over-worked muscles protested as Lyla tried to lean back against the smooth trunk of the tree. She tried to turn her wince into a toothy grin. "I'm a little sore," she confessed after another look of worry crossed Gabby's face.

"Show me." It sounded like a command, but Lyla knew it was a question. If Gabby had better control of her words, the tone wouldn't have sounded so stern. As soon as she pointed to the ache in her shoulders, Gabby pressed her fingertips into the sore muscles, working the knots out.

Lyla moaned. It hurt, but in a good way. The softness and warmth of Gabby's fingers left a tingling in Lyla's core that she tried her best to ignore. She wanted to flip Gabby on her back and worship her with her tongue, lapping at her sweet nectar. Under completely different circumstances, this could've counted as a very romantic outing. Unfortunately, they were trying their best to not get caught on their way back to safety. Lyla couldn't keep Gabby safe if she was distracted, no matter how delicious that distraction was.

A small flock of mismatched birds soared overhead, catching Lyla's attention. Lyla shielded her eyes from the harsh sun to try to tell their size or type, but they were too far away to make out any details. "Do you think they're ASS scouts or more goons from Dr. Grimm?" She pointed them out to Gabby before they disappeared beyond the edge of the orchard.

Gabby shook her head, her untamed hair bouncing over her shoulders. "Don't know." She was squinting up at the blue sky when a twig snapped a handful of trees away from them. Lyla's attention snapped toward the sound. *No. Not again.* The flight had left her too drained to fight. She didn't even think she could manage standing, let alone walking or fighting.

13

Lyla shuddered under Gabby's fingers when the shrew shifter stepped into view. He still wore the clothes he had on in the parking lot by the park, so he must have been following them on foot. But how? She didn't know enough about shrews to know why Dr. Grimm said he was good at finding things.

Bile rose in the back of Gabby's throat. She was sick of being hunted and even sicker of being scared. She glanced at Lyla. The shock had blanched her skin, a pale comparison to her vibrant hair. Gabby could tell by looking at her that Lyla had pushed herself too far. It was Gabby's turn to protect Lyla, to pay her back in kind for rescuing her in the parking lot.

Gabby crawled out from under the limbs of the apple tree for fear of catching her wings again. She wasn't used to the damn things, and they extended her height by a couple of feet. She stood after clearing the boughs, stretching her wings out. The span of them was incredible, a good seven feet at least in either direction. If the shrew thought she was an easy target as a crow, what would he think of her now?

"Gabby." The shrew somehow knew her name. He held his hands out as if to show he was unarmed. "It's nothing personal."

"Personal?" The word caught in her throat like a piece of unchewed food. Gabby scoffed at his soft tone and polite demeanor. Why did he seem apologetic every time he saw her? In her room, he apologized in advance before capturing her. In the parking lot, he assured her he wouldn't hurt her. Now "it's nothing personal." What kidnapper walked around in a polo shirt and khakis anyway?

She narrowed her eyes at the man who wouldn't give up tracking her. He'd found her at WANC and then again near the park. "How?" she found herself asking. She wanted to know how he was able to keep popping up when she stopped running.

He sighed, rolling his shoulders forward as if exhausted. He reached a hand into the pocket of his clean pants, pulling out a small device the size of a smartphone. "Dr. Grimm put a tracking device in the back of your neck."

"He what?" She reached for the back of her neck, pushing the sweat-drenched hair away. After rubbing her palm across her skin, she felt it. A small bump. And cleverly placed where her hair would hide it.

Anger ripped through her body, more powerful than what she'd felt in her cell yesterday. She wanted her life back. She was so sick of hiding. Of wondering if Dr. Grimm was lurking around every corner. She flapped her wings in the direction of the shrew shifter, sending a powerful gust of wind his way. He fell backward, stumbling onto his ass.

Small twigs cut into the soles of Gabby's feet as she stomped toward him. He would pay for what he stole from her. If it weren't for him, Dr. Grimm wouldn't have turned her into whatever she now was. Dr. Grimm had not only fucked with her but he'd fucked with her family as well. Her dad struggled to stay human and could hardly talk. She could barely carry on a conversation herself. And Phin... Look what visiting her and her dad did to Phin each time. Her brother was barely holding it together. All this heartbreak and pain was caused by them.

The man crab-crawled, trying to increase the distance between them, but Gabby was too fast. She picked him up by the neck. Heat seared her skin, the anger burning her up from the inside. It buzzed in her chest and heated her face. "Why?" She squeezed, tightening her grip.

The man clawed at her fingers, but she could barely feel it. Fear filled his green eyes as he struggled to breathe, but she couldn't let go. His neck felt so delicate and fragile under her fingers. How easy it would be to snap it like a twig and end this, freeing Gabby from fear forever. True, he wasn't Dr. Grimm, but the shrew was a part of it. She wanted her life back, but more than that, she wanted someone to pay for what was done to her and the others. She didn't care who was punished, as long as someone was. She gritted her teeth, feeling the pressure mount in her jaw as her hate rose like waves of a typhoon.

A soft, clammy hand touched the back of her arm. "Gabby?" She turned to see tears streaking down Lyla's face. Gabby crumpled, her knees giving out, letting go of the man, who fell to the ground with a hollow thud. He sputtered for breath, rubbing the red skin of his neck as Lyla wrapped her arms around Gabby. Gabby nuzzled into her neck, smelling her sweet and comforting scent. Her waves of anger broke against the shelter of Lyla's compassion and warmth. Gabby wanted this nightmare to end, but at what cost? She'd almost sold her soul to finish it.

"It's okay." Lyla stoked Gabby's hair as Gabby's tears soaked her neck. Gabby couldn't hold them in anymore. The floodgates of her grief sprang open as she grieved for the life she'd lost. She would never be the same after this.

"Furry United Coalition!" someone shouted as a group converged in on them. "Put your hands where we can see them!"

They all did as they were told, though the agents only pointed their guns at the man in khakis. He looked up at the women as he was being cuffed. "He has my sister."

14

"Anson, the shrew shifter, is cooperating. His scent is the same as the intruder I was tracking earlier. I lost the trail on the side of the street, so we assumed he parked his vehicle there and snuck onto campus," Agent Stone assured Gabby as the evening nurse, Mya, took her vitals. She looked to the agents, noting the tension between Agent Stone and his partner, Agent Sparks. The ASS agent seemed wound up tighter than the red curls framing her face. Her hazel eyes shifted to Agent Stone's face briefly before she tapped her stiletto toe on the floor impatiently. There was something they weren't telling her, and Agent Sparks didn't seem to agree with Agent Stone keeping that information to himself. Her red lips formed a thin line, as if keeping them tightly together was the only way to stay quiet.

"But?" Gabby raised an eyebrow at them, daring them to tell her what she already assumed. Dr. Grimm was lost to the wind, or whatever that expression was. Hiding the truth from Gabby would do nothing to protect her. She would bet money that Agent Sparks understood that.

The agents exchanged looks, engaging in some sort of

silent argument. Eventually Agent Stone rolled his eyes, giving in.

"The lab where Anson said they took you is already empty," Agent Sparks confessed as she brushed a coil of curly red hair out of her face.

"You didn't"—Gabby swallowed and focused on her next words—"find his sister?" Gabby remembered the look of desperation on the shrew's—Anson's—face before the agents came to the rescue. The mix-and-match bird flock was a group of ASS agents scouting the nearby area for the women or anything suspicious. An eagle shifter—ASS Agent Lee— was able to spot the pair and the man moving in on their position. Agent Lee called in for backup. Then the ground agents came in.

Without Lyla being there, Gabby shuddered to think what she would have done to Anson. Anger and hate had blinded her. Some would think she had every right to take out what Dr. Grimm did to her on Anson. But could she really hate a brother who was just doing what he needed to? He was just like Phin. Phin did everything he could to find Gabby last year.

She shuddered to think how Sandy and Dr. Grimm could have used her brother if they'd gotten to him before Agents Stone and Sparks had. The roles could have been reversed, and Phin could have ended up a henchman of Sandy and Dr. Grimm, forced to carry out their will with the hopes of getting his sister back. Maybe the fact that he was so young helped. Perhaps he didn't appear useful to the evil scientists. Whatever the reason, Gabby thanked her lucky stars that they didn't try to use Phin like that.

"No," Agent Stone said softly, bringing Gabby out of her thoughts "But we're going to keep looking."

After asking her to reach out with any helpful information she could recall in the coming days, the agents wished Gabby well and headed out.

While Dr. Grimm was still on the loose, Gabby didn't feel the fear like she did before. It was in one part because FUC knew about him now. They were actively looking for him. But there was another reason: whatever the doctor did to her, she was much stronger than before. She'd knocked Anson back with just the flap of her new wings. Let the doctor find her now. She'd tear him from limb to limb.

"Penny for your thoughts?" Lyla leaned against the door to Gabby's hospital room. Her trusty IV bag rolled up next to her.

Gabby stifled a giggle. A miniature tuxedo jacket wrapped around the dextrose drip bag, complete with a white under-shirt and matching black bowtie. Lyla turned to look, a pink blush matching her hair creeping up her cheeks. "Well, I know he wasn't invited to the party, but if I go, he has to go as well. Char was helping me with a tux fitting."

"I like," Gabby said, causing Lyla's face to light up with a wide grin.

Only Lyla would think of dressing up her IV bag for the party, and Gabby loved her for that. They might be stuck in the hospital for longer than they originally would have been, but they were going to make the best of each moment. Especially since it was the day before Huggie's big shindig, and both Lyla and Gabby were medically cleared to attend.

"So… what had you looking so pensive a moment ago?" Lyla asked, stepping into the room—IV pole in tow—and taking a seat on the bed next to Lyla.

"Phin," Gabby admitted. "What if Sandy…" Talking was getting easier as long as she kept her emotions at bay. She took a deep breath, centering herself, finding her words. "How awful if they…" Gabby gulped. Lyla watched her with round hazel eyes, patiently letting her finish the thought. "Used Phin. Like Dr. Grimm… with Anson."

Pain filled Lyla's eyes. Gabby had learned that Lyla had many brothers and sisters, so the thought would be effortless for her to empathize with. It very easily could have been either one of their siblings in Anson's place. And it was easy to imagine what they wouldn't have done to get the evil doctor to release their loved one… Gabby shuddered at the thought.

She scratched at the bandage on the back of her neck. The adhesive pulled her hair when she turned her head. While she was glad to be rid of the tracking device, she couldn't wait to remove the bandage. She winced after touching the still-tender incision.

Lyla pulled Gabby's hand away from the wound. "Leave it."

Gabby crossed her arms across her chest. It was hard to not scratch it. Restless energy bubbled up in her. She was scheduled to visit with her family later. While the agents had notified them of her new changes, Gabby wasn't sure how it would go. They'd been through so much already.

As if reading her mind, Lyla tried to put her at ease. "They will love you no matter what. This won't break them." She put a soft reassuring hand on Gabby's arm.

Gabby nodded. Lyla was right. Aside from the cut on her neck when the doctors of WANC removed the tracking device, there wasn't a mark on Gabby—except for the wings. But they didn't really count as a wound since all the injuries from them developing had healed. They were just new—and a complication toward her re-entering society anytime soon, since they were so very hard to miss.

But she was working on getting used to life with them. Gabby found the most difficult part of living with them was trying to get cozy in bed. There was a reason birds slept on their bellies, nestled into their nests. Gabby considered shifting before bedtime so that she could sleep more comfortably.

That wasn't all. Even getting through doorways had proven to be a challenge. That was a feat by itself. Gabby kept forgetting to tuck her wings in as she was ushered through the hospital halls earlier. She clipped her wings on every doorframe she crossed. They would take some getting used to. Maybe one day she'd muster the courage to fly with them, though it would have to be limited to the airspace over FUCN'A so that no humans saw her.

Lynn popped her head into Gabby's room, one pencil behind her ear and one in her mouth. "Are you ready?" she asked between chomps on the wood. Gabby didn't think it was a good sign if Lynn felt she needed two pencils to chew on during her family meeting. Anxiety roiled the nausea in her gut.

"You got this." Lyla put a hand on Gabby's shoulder, reassuring her with a smile as if reading her thoughts.

That was enough to help Gabby feel she could accomplish anything, even another visit with her family.

"Would you…come with…with me?" Gabby asked, wondering if it was too soon to invite Lyla. The two hadn't exactly put a label on what they were. Did it count as dating if they technically hadn't gone on a first date yet?

To her relief, Lyla wasn't taken aback by the offer. "I'd love to." A warm smile brightened her face.

Introducing Lyla to her family should have been a big deal, but unfortunately, her wings took the spotlight.

"You look badass!" Phin proclaimed, his face lighting up with excitement. "Like a superhero."

"Phin, don't swear," Kristin chastised him, though her worried expression hardly changed. They'd been warned of Gabby's change before she'd arrived, but still, her mother's glassy eyes scanned the wings as if trying to see whether it was some sort of prank, like a costume piece strapped to Gabby's back instead of the new bone, flesh, and feathers jutting out. Being young, Phin probably didn't fully understand Gabby's new limitations. She would never fit into a human community again. Not unless the doctors figured out a way to reverse the transformation or a way that she could shift the wings away when needed. Both of which she doubted.

"Wings." Joe scanned Gabby's new appendages, though he didn't appear as worried as Kristin. He smiled at his daughter, his blue eyes lighting up with pride. "Still beautiful."

"I agree," Lyla said, drawing a blush to Gabby's cheeks. She smiled warmly at Gabby's family in greeting.

This seemed to draw both parents' attention to the additional visitor. "This is Lyla," Gabby managed to say. Butterflies churned in her stomach. She hoped her family liked Lyla as much as she did.

"It's nice to meet you, Lyla. Please, have a seat," Kristin said, patting the couch next to her. She welcomed her with a grin.

"You're... patient... too?" Joe asked.

"I am," Lyla confirmed with a nod. "Hopefully once I get my energy back and they figure out the feather problem"—she waved at the pink feathers in her hair—"I'll be able to leave."

"Survived Sandy. Like us," Gabby said, sitting on the other couch, next to her father, careful her wings didn't bump into him.

"You're safe." Joe pulled Gabby in for a hug, squeezing her hard. "All that matters." It felt good that Dad was able to wrap his strong arms around her again. It had been so long since he'd been able to embrace her.

"Maybe you could take me flying one day?" Phin clearly thought this was the coolest thing ever. She didn't fault him for it though. And his positive view of her change helped lighten her mood a little.

Gabby glanced at her parents. Neither one of them would be okay with that. Even if she got used to her new appendages, they wouldn't let her take Phin more than a few feet off the ground for fear he'd somehow fall. "Maybe." She wasn't sure what else to say. She glanced to her mom, hoping for some help.

"She may not be able to fly with them, honey. Gabby hasn't tried yet. They might not support her weight. And she has more recovering to do before the doctors will let her try." Mom with the perfect non-committed, vague answer. Kristin made saying no without really saying no an art form.

"Flying isn't all it's cracked up to be. I hear you're a mouse shifter. That's pretty cool! Do you like cheese?" Lyla perfectly changed the subject.

Phin chuckled. "Why does everyone ask me that?" Lyla smoothed it over with a shrug as a sheepish look crossed her face.

"Huggie's party?" Joe asked, with a raised eyebrow, glancing from Lyla to Gabby. Though he couldn't fully say all the words he needed to, he was getting good at using non-verbal communication to assist.

"Yes. With date." Gabby nodded toward Lyla while beaming. She was happy to share this news with them. The excitement bubbled up inside her, bringing a wide grin to her face. Her joyful words cut through the tense mood of the room.

"Wait. You're a bird, too?" Phin asked Lyla.

"Yes. I'm a hummingbird." She grinned, brightening up her beautiful face.

"Hummingbirds are small, like me!" Phin said, clearly pleased. "But I wish I had wings."

"Wish I had whiskers." It was Gabby's usual response to when her brother felt left out when she and her dad would bond over being crow shifters, even though Kristin and Phin had plenty of fun adventures together as mice. She pulled him in for a hug.

"I love you, sis."

"Love you." Despite the last twenty-four hours, Gabby felt all was right in the world. Dr. Grimm was still on the loose, but he'd given her new strength, and he'd be an idiot to try to capture her again. Hopefully, Anson would prove useful in tracking him down. Dr. Grimm said the shrew had a talent for that. Maybe he'd use it for good instead of evil.

Gabby beamed at her family. They weren't perfect, yet at the same time, they were. They were just what she needed. And wait a minute… She turned to her dad, who still sat on the couch in his human form, legs dangling over the side and feet planted on the floor. "Not crow?"

Joe smiled. "Control it… better."

Gabby's eyes stung with tears. For the first time in a year, her father wasn't struggling to stay in human form. Earlier this week, he'd made it only a few minutes. "How?" It didn't seem possible.

He shrugged. "Just clicked."

Just like how Lynn helped her to talk better, to tap into the part of her brain used for singing. Gabby found it easier to follow the thread, keep the sentence strung together. Maybe not all the time, but more often than she had before. Not every day would be perfect, but they were getting better. No one could deny that. Lyla gently squeezed her arm and smiled. Even she knew what a big step that was.

15

———————

Lyla nibbled on some of the hors d'oeuvres that Huggie had put out for the party. She was thrilled to find chocolate-covered strawberries on a tray at a long table covered in snacks and goodies. Various people she noticed during her stay at the hospital mingled in groups around the cafeteria, some enjoying the food as well. Lyla got a few chuckles over the tux on her IV bag. She just shrugged her shoulders. She was stuck with the dextrose drip again for who knew how long. Might as well make the best of it. Although she noticed she was feeling better quicker than when she'd first been brought into the hospital. Maybe her situation had improved.

Huggie went all out with the decorations. Lyla was pleased to see the cafeteria transformed. Colorful streamers and balloons were taped up in bundles around the room. It felt like a high school dance. Not that Lyla had gone to many, but she saw them in TV shows. This is just how she imagined they'd be in real life.

She flattened out the front of the hand-me-down dress her mother got her from one of her older cousins. Lyla could not believe she found one in her favorite color: pink. Her parents couldn't afford the nicest things, but they always found the most thoughtful of items. Like the dress she now wore. She adjusted one of the spaghetti straps before taking a cup of punch from Char. The tiny pink pouch with drawstrings, which she'd made, swung on her wrist with the motion. Her tiny pebble rested safely inside.

As if noting Lyla's gaze kept going to the door, Char reminded her, "She'll be here soon. Lynn and her mom were helping her get ready." Char didn't have to say who she was referring to. The whole hospital seemed to know Gabby and Lyla were an item. Not that they did anything to hide it.

Lyla's breath caught in her throat as she glanced at the door as Gabby entered. A stunning black dress stretched across her curvy frame. The plunge neckline showed off her ample breasts, the very ones Lyla had explored with her tongue last night.

Gabby twirled after entering the room, showing off the backless dress. Her wings seemed a part of the outfit, covering what the dress didn't of Gabby's back. They shimmered in the colorful lights, reflecting hues of green, blue, and purple.

The miniature tux on the IV bag fluttered as Lyla ran toward Gabby, her pink heels clacking on the floor. She threw her arms around Gabby, careful to not pull the IV line out of her hand. "You look beautiful." She pressed her lips to Gabby's, melting into her body. The world around them dissolved. Lyla's heartbeat quickened, thrumming a hypnotic rhythm in her ear. Her stomach twisted in knots, but in a good way. Her core heated. The world felt right when their bodies touched. Their passion made her soul sing.

Gabby cupped the back of Lyla's head, pulling her closer. Lyla's tongue met Gabby's, gently exploring her mouth. She tasted so good and sweeter than the chocolate-covered strawberries. Every part of her was the rarest nectar. Absolutely delectable. Lyla couldn't believe it took her so long to get up the nerve to ask the woman out. Not only was she sexy but she was also a good friend. She never left Lyla feeling imperfect or forgotten. Lyla shuddered to think what would have happened had Gabby not been able to escape from Dr. Grimm.

"Look nice," Gabby said after pulling herself away from Lyla long enough to take in her dress.

Lyla's eyes scanned Gabby's body, pausing briefly over her exceptional curves. Lyla knew their minds were in the same place, a very naughty one.

"You too."

Hell, that was an understatement. The woman looked good enough to eat. If there was a closet in the cafeteria, she'd have half a mind to sneak off with Gabby and do all the sensual things she didn't get to do the other day. Her panties dampened at the visual her brain created. Heat flooded her cheeks. She ran a finger up Gabby's bare back.

"At least dresses are easier to fit into." She knew Gabby stressed over finding clothes that would accommodate her wings.

"Can't always… wear dresses." She rolled her eyes at the thought.

"Why not? You look pretty good in them." Lyla laced her fingers through Gabby's. Gabby squeezed her hand, but her mind appeared elsewhere. "Are you okay?"

Gabby sighed before flicking her blue eyes from the door back to Lyla's. "Part of me… feels safe. Another part…" Her worried eyes found the open doorway leading from the cafeteria to the hall. "Worries that… Anson or Grimm… will come." She sighed and breathed deeply between words, working her way through the sentence like an explorer hacking their way through the jungle.

Lyla gave her a hug. "You just went through something

traumatic… like yesterday. You have to be patient with yourself."

"Two days."

"Whatever." Now it was Lyla's turn to roll her eyes. "Of course you'll worry. Who wouldn't?" She wanted to add she worried, too, but was afraid Gabby would feel invalidated, like she was brushing off Gabby's feelings or something. Instead, she offered a reassuring smile.

"I'm stronger, though." Gabby's wings flared slightly.

Lyla wondered if it was on purpose or on accident. Gabby was still learning to control her new limbs. Lyla couldn't even imagine how challenging that must've been.

"It's okay to be scared. It doesn't mean you're not strong."

A wide smile brightened Gabby's face. "Phin would say that."

"And Phin's a smart little boy."

"He is."

Lyla gently took Gabby's hand and planted a kiss on it. "And every ASS agent is watching Anson like…well, a hawk. He's not going to try anything. And now that they know about Dr. Grimm, I bet he won't be on the run for long."

Gabby shrugged. Her face said she wasn't convinced.

Lyla wished there was something she could do to make Gabby feel better. She hated feeling so helpless. Then she remembered her pebble. It had become like a safety blanket for her, giving her courage when she needed it most.

"I have something that will help." Lyla slid the pink drawstrings from around her wrist and handed the small pouch to Gabby. "My lucky pebble is inside. It sounds dumb, but it helped me get through some really hard times. I want you to have it."

Gabby's eyes glistened as she took the pouch. "I couldn't…"

"I want you to have it. Plus crows like pebbles, don't they?"

"Yes, but… it's yours."

"And now it's yours." Lyla smiled. She'd never put much stock into lucky charms until she needed that pebble. It felt right to give it to Gabby. Lyla glanced to the busy dance floor. "What do you say we pretend, just for tonight, that we are two normal people who've never heard of Sandy or Dr. Grimm? They don't deserve to take up our headspace. Not tonight… not ever."

Gabby nodded, sliding the drawstring pouch with the pebble around her wrist. "Let's dance!"

Anson struggled to get his pant leg over the ankle monitor FUC and ASS forced him to wear. Though they seemed to believe his story, they didn't fully trust him. Who could blame them? He'd broken into WANC and birdnapped a patient.

The thought of going back to Dr. Grimm for help was tempting. But the more he thought of it, the less sense it made. The whole time he worked for that psycho, he hardly got a glimpse of his sister. If he wanted her back, he'd have to play FUC and ASS's game. He hated following the rules. Shortcuts were always more fun. That's why he embedded the tracker in Gabby. He needed to keep an eye on Dr. Grimm's prize. Plus being a shrew shifter meant he could do a lot of things very quickly. Did his sensitive whiskers or his speed make it easier for him to find whatever Dr. Grimm needed? He wasn't sure. He just knew he was good at it. His mind went back to his sister, Ariel. Too bad he couldn't find her on his own. If he had foreseen Ariel being captured, Anson would've put a tracker in her as well.

He jumped as a knock sounded on his hotel room door, breaking through his thoughts. He put his eye up to the peephole. "Shit."

A slim woman in jeans and a plain T-shirt stood at the door, looking like a statue placed in the middle of the hall. Though she wasn't tall, she stood straight and rigid, seemingly taking up all the space the corridor had to offer. This lady was like a bad penny. She attended every interrogation, standing in the corner watching him with her eagle eyes. What she saw when she looked at him, Anson didn't know. With a huff, he opened the door. She wouldn't leave until she got what she came for.

"Agent Lee. What can I—"

She barged in without letting him finish. Agent Lee pushed her long, silky black hair over her shoulder to keep it out of her face. She narrowed her brown eyes at him. "The other agents may trust you, but I sure as hell don't."

"It's not like I can go anywhere." Anson pointed to the ankle with the device locked around it. "The monitor sends you my position every five minutes. If I shift, this thing will notify you immediately." He hated suspicious people. He found them annoying. Especially the ones who thought they knew everything. This agent knew nothing about him, though her piercing gaze said otherwise.

Agent Lee pulled something out of her pocket. Anson jumped, assuming it was a weapon. Maybe she was an assassin sent by Dr. Grimm. He wouldn't doubt it. Dude had no morals.

"Relax." She crouched down, lifting his pant leg to inspect the device. After a few clicks, it fell to the ground. "Unless you want every FUC and ASS agent to pounce on you in the next ten minutes, I suggest we leave."

He stared at her. She was super hot, but was she just as

psycho, too? And what kind of an ASS agent would free him like this? "I don't understand."

"You can stand here like the coward you are, or you can help me find Dr. Grimm."

"Coward?" He raised an eyebrow at her. Working next to that psycho to try to save his sister made him anything but in his opinion.

"You should have told the authorities about Dr. Grimm." Nari crossed her arms, narrowing her brown eyes to slits.

"Well, it's not that easy. He said if I involved any FUC or ASS agents, he'd mutate my sister so badly, I wouldn't be able to recognize her." Saying it aloud stung. The thought kept him awake at night, wondering if the worst had already been done to her. He pressed the sadness down into his core, ignoring it. He couldn't help his sister if he fell apart.

A somber look crossed Nari's face. Was that maybe even a shred of compassion? As quickly as it came, the look vanished. She cocked her head sideways, taking him in. "Are you going to help me or not?"

"Why?" He stared at the ankle monitor on the ground.

"Because we're all given the choice to do things the right way or the quick way. Make your choice. I'm leaving." Without another word ASS Agent—former ASS Agent, apparently—Lee opened the door, leaving him to his thoughts.

He had no time to think. He didn't like being on the run, but he liked worrying about what Dr. Grimm could be doing to his sister even less. He'd witnessed enough of the creep's twisted experiments to know what the freak was capable of. Without another thought, Anson grabbed his wallet and followed Nari Lee.

The End

Or is it? Stay tuned for Anson and Nari's story, coming in The Eagle and the Shrew, by Scarlet Fox (releasing summer 2025)!

And there are more FUC Academy books from other authors coming your way!

To find out more about these books and more, visit worlds.EveLanglais.com or sign up for the EveL Worlds newsletter. If you haven't already downloaded the **free Academy intro** (written by Eve Langlais) make sure you grab it at worlds.evelanglais.com/wordpress/book/fucacademy1!

Shadow Cat and the Sloth

A great outdoors adventure might be more than this cat and sloth bargained for.

Ellie Talbot is a cadet at FUCN'A after being rescued from an experimental lab. She was once human and now can shift into a black cat. Oh, and she can also bend light waves around her to turn herself invisible. NBD.

The shadow cat is thrilled to hear that her technical training class will be in the field for survivalist training… until she hears who she's assigned to partner with.

Brett Kipp's sweet sloth smile is nothing short of a ray of sunshine, but that doesn't help Ellie's confidence in his survival abilities. Add in the fact that part of their training includes river rapids, and this trip is no longer the cat's meow.

The Hound and the Peacock

She's a peahen, not a peacock, thank you very much!

Grayson Stone thought his days in the field were over, but when FUC needs one of their best hunters and trackers on the job, he can't say no. The complication he wasn't expecting? The Avian Soaring Society sending a certain crested beauty to partner with him on this mission. Now, between tracking down baddies and sniffing out clues, the hound will have to deal with the most high-maintenance bird he's ever crossed paths with.

ASS agent Cassandra Sparks knows Grayson won't be happy to see her, but forgetting what they had together has been impossible. Now she's heading to the academy to find and capture a hawk-at-large, and convince her old flame that she's turned over a new feather.

ABOUT THE AUTHOR

Scarlet Fox (aka B.L. Carroll) enjoys writing when she isn't at her day job. Creating romances is a fun challenge for her. Scarlet's alter ego loves writing mysteries and supernatural thrillers with a strong female lead. Destigmatizing mental health and other internal struggles are recurring themes in her fiction. Other hobbies include painting, singing, or going for walks. Coffee is a necessity, as is reading. She lives in western New York with her fur babies and partner.

Please visit her website for other titles and information. Thank you for reading!

Website: scarletfoxauthor.wixsite.com

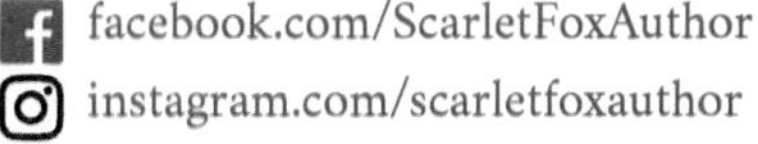

facebook.com/ScarletFoxAuthor
instagram.com/scarletfoxauthor

www.ingramcontent.com/pod-product-compliance
Lightning Source LLC
Chambersburg PA
CBHW021010160726
47994CB00006B/2451